MW00738010

Homeland Security

The Beginning

Written by Paul P. Lubianetzky

PublishAmerica
Baltimore

© 2008 by Paul P. Lubianetzky.
All rights reserved. No part of this book may be reproduced, stored in a retrieval system or transmitted in any form or by any means without the prior written permission of the publishers, except by a reviewer who may quote brief passages in a review to be printed in a newspaper, magazine or journal.

First printing

All characters in this book are fictitious, and any resemblance to real persons, living or dead, is coincidental.

ISBN: 1-60563-585-5
PUBLISHED BY PUBLISHAMERICA, LLLP
www.publishamerica.com
Baltimore

Printed in the United States of America

Enjoy your right to read.

Paul P. Sachett

12/18/08

This book was written for entertainment with the hope that free people everywhere will become more aware and ever vigilant to the possible dangers to their freedoms from an overzealous government's ability to erode civil rights in the name of keeping its citizens safe.

Introduction

Sometime during Adolph Hitler's infamous reign, he coined the slogan, "Heute Deutschland, morgen die Welt!" "Today Germany, tomorrow the world!" Some religions, including Christianity, believe in evil spirits influencing people to commit evil deeds. They support this idea by citing accounts of such happenings in the Bible. Many Christians believe that Adolph Hitler was possessed by the devil himself; who convinced him that he would conquer the world if he could only eliminate the Jews. Hence, over six million Jews were murdered! The German people allowed these atrocities to happen because Hitler brought Germany out of a severe depression by blaming the Jews and confiscating their wealth. He gave the German people a false feeling of security by building a huge military machine and promising them a thousand-year reign by Germany over the world. They paid for this security by allowing the civil rights of the Jews, and people related to Jews, to deteriorate to the point of non-existence. Because of this deterioration of the civil rights of one group of people, the German people unwittingly became enslaved themselves: enslaved to the ideology of Nazism. They had no mind of their own; all that mattered was what their leader thought and said. It has been said that something like Nazi Germany could never happen here. The American people would never allow it. Yet, we have allowed warrantless wiretaps, warrantless searches, warrantless interception of private email, and secret prisons abroad.

On April 30, 1945, Hitler committed suicide in his bunker in Berlin; thus ending the 1,000-year reign approximately 986 years early. It's theologized that whatever possessed him, if one believes in such

5

things, left his body at the point of death, and went searching for another host. If you believe in this theory; then you can read this book in context with your beliefs.

If you do not believe in evil spirits and the like; then you can read this book as a very possible look into the future. For the future is governed by the past. In the words of the philosopher and poet George Santayana (Born Dec. 16, 1863, Died Sept. 26, 1952):

"Those who cannot remember the past are condemned to repeat it."

Chapter One

It was a beautiful spring day. Brad and Mary Spencer stood looking at their recently purchased home at 1932 Oak Street. Even though they've been married for almost three years, they felt like newlyweds.

"Are you sure we did the right thing?" Mary asked.

"Sure I'm sure," Brad replied. "I'll admit this house needs a little work, but the way property values are going up in this area, we'll double our purchase price in five years!"

Mary countered with, "I don't know. There is more to do than just a little work. The windows are cracked, the roof leaks, the paint is almost non-existent, and that's just the outside."

Brad reassured her with, "Hey, so I'll have to work nights and weekends for a couple of months. It'll be worth it in the end. Besides, I love you, and we'll be working together. That's all that matters to me."

Mary looked at the man she married after a two-year engagement. She reviewed the reasons why she married him in about ten seconds. How a woman can do that is beyond any man's comprehension. He's hardworking, honest, and completely trustworthy, never forgets a birthday or anniversary, cute, great hair, neat, clean, slim, and the cutest buns she's ever seen. What's not to love?

She answered, "I love you too, and if you say we can do it, then we will!"

Well, it took slightly longer than a couple of months, like about six months and twenty thousand dollars longer! The end results were worth it though. The night they declared the house project finished would be indelibly etched in Brad's memory forever. He took a shower after work, put on a suit and tie, and walked into the dining room. There was Mary lighting the candles and looking more beautiful, if that were possible, than the day he met her. When she looked at him and smiled, nothing else mattered in the world but their love. He felt so lucky to have such a beautiful woman for his wife. Before sitting down, he pulled her chair out and seated her. During dinner they talked about the ups and downs of remodeling the house. They both agreed on one thing. They were both glad it was over. After dinner, they snuggled up by the fireplace with a glass of sparkling grape juice and just watched the fire. After a while, Brad looked deep into Mary's eyes and told her how much he loved her and kissed her. Then, they went hand in hand to the bedroom and made the most incredible love Brad had ever experienced.

The next morning, they enjoyed a breakfast of half a grapefruit, oatmeal with brown sugar and milk, and a cup of green tea. As Brad was leaving for work, Mary kissed him and said, "Last night was incredible. I have never felt closer to anyone in my entire life."

Brad held her in his arms and said, "You mean more to me than life itself. Mary, I will love you forever."

Brad stepped outside the kitchen door and took a deep breath of the cool fall air. The leaves on the trees had turned to vibrant red, orange, and yellow, and were brilliantly illuminated by the morning sun. Squirrels were running back and forth, collecting and burying acorns for the coming winter. Life couldn't get any better than this. Getting into his pickup, he started the commute to work. He pulled into the parking lot and parked his pickup beneath the sign that read, "Best Cable Service." Then, he checked out his pristine classic 1976 pickup like he always did. He'd been doing this same routine every workday for the past five years. Brad was a computer and electronics technician in the service with cross-training in special operations. When he got out of the Army, civilian companies wouldn't recognize his military training; so he had to settle for a cable guy job. Actually the pay wasn't bad and he got to meet all kinds of people, so he didn't mind. Two years ago, he enrolled in a computer and electronics course at the local college. His goal was to get a degree and move up to an even better-paying job.

Brad opened the employee entrance door, walked over to the time clock, and clocked in. Then he walked over to the shift supervisor's desk and picked up his work orders. The shift supervisor, Tom Demarco, has been Brad's supervisor for five years. He's kind of a quiet guy for a supervisor.

"Hey, Brad!" A loud voice broke Brad's line of thought about today's work orders. It was Jim Rathburn. Mary and Brad had gone to dinner with Jim and his wife a couple of times at Jim's insistence. Brad couldn't say they were friends. Jim was the kind of guy that Brad was on a first-name basis with, but not much more.

"Brad, did you hear the news?" Jim said excitedly.

"What news?" Brad asked.

"Congress just passed a bill banning satellite TV receivers in the United States!"

"What? They can't do that!" Brad answered.

"Maybe not, but they did. You know what that means don't you? We're going to have a whole lot more customers and installations. Talk about job security!"

"What reason could they possibly have for doing that?" Brad asked. It was at that moment that Jim reminded Brad why they were just barely above acquaintance status.

Jim answered, "How the hell should I know? All I read is the headlines. Here, you read the rest for yourself."

Thrusting the morning paper against Brad's chest; Jim turned on his heels and headed for his assigned service truck. Brad looked at his watch and started for his service truck and his first appointment. The paper would have to wait until lunchtime.

The morning went smoothly. There were no real problems with any of Brad's stops. He was amazed that so many people had little or no comment about the congressional act banning satellite TV receivers. That could be because his customers were cable people already. Even so, he thought that they would be concerned about not having the right to choose. Anyway, it was 12:30 p.m. and time for lunch. Since Brad didn't eat fast food, he stopped at a nearby park to use the restroom and wash his hands. He opened his lunch consisting of a lettuce and alfalfa sprout sandwich and a handful of baby carrots. Then he started reading the article about the ban on satellite receivers.

The article read like something out of a bad spy story. The vote passing the bill went through both houses of Congress even faster than the Patriot Act passed on October 24, 2001. Apparently, the Department of Homeland Security originally initiated the reason for the ban on satellite TV receivers. This was kept secret from the press and the general public until now. It probably never would have come to light if it weren't for an unnamed source in the DHS. It seems the DHS is afraid terrorists are using overseas programs originating in the Middle East to transmit secret instructions to terrorists in the U.S. So, with the ban on receivers, the information being transmitted would be stopped. Existing cable companies don't carry such programs and if they would decide to do so, the new law forbids it. The president is expected to sign the new bill into law within twenty-four hours. The article also went on to say that the satellite TV companies would undoubtedly challenge the ban before the Supreme Court.

Brad couldn't believe what he had just read. Free enterprise is the backbone of this country, and to say a company is not allowed to transmit a program is a violation of the first amendment to the Constitution. To put a company out of business for doing so violates too many constitutional laws to mention.

"Oh well, the Supreme Court will put a stop to it. That's why the founding fathers established a system of checks and balances in our government in the first place," Brad reasoned.

Brad looked at his watch. He had just enough time to get to his next appointment. So he finished his sandwich, took a slug of filtered water, and pulled out of the parking lot.

Mary left for work about five minutes after Brad. She stopped at a convenience store, as usual, and picked up a morning newspaper. The headline about the ban on satellite receivers immediately caught her eye. She wouldn't read it right away, although she was very interested. There would be plenty of time for that when she got to school. Mary has been a high school civics teacher for ten years. She laid the paper on the seat next to her and pulled out into traffic for her short commute to work.

Mary arrived at the high school, as she did most mornings, about forty-five minutes before her first class. She drove into the faculty parking lot and parked in her parking space. Mary walked into the faculty entrance and stopped by the school office. She said hello to Jane, the secretary, engaged in a little small talk, picked up her mail from her box, and walked down to the teachers' lounge. Mary opened the door and looked around.

She said, "Good morning, everyone," as usual, and as usual, they said, "Good morning, Mary," and went back to complaining to each other about everything from the cafeteria food to misbehaving students.

Mary went down the hall to her classroom. She opened the door and went inside to her desk, where she opened her mail and started to read the article on the ban of satellite receivers. After finishing the article, she was astonished that anything like this could happen in the United States of America.

"Have we become so paranoid about terrorism that we are now willing to sacrifice our civil rights in the name of keeping our people and country safe? How safe are we, if we give the powers that be the authority to tell us what we can or can't watch? What's next? Will they be telling us what to read and what not to read? Oh, what am I worried about? I'm sure the Supreme Court will nip this new law in the bud," Mary reassured herself.

The bell ringing and her first class of the day slowly filing in put an end to her thoughts.

Mary arrived home after work a full two hours before Brad. That's one of the perks of being a schoolteacher. If there's no teachers' meeting after school, she gets home early. About 4:30 p.m. she started making dinner. Mary enjoyed cooking and was glad that she and Brad agreed on a healthy diet. Tonight, she was preparing a fresh vegetable soup and salad with whole-wheat bread. Brad came home about 5:30 p.m. He gave Mary a "Hi, honey" and a kiss before he went up to the bathroom to clean up for dinner. They sat down to dinner a few minutes later.

Mary said, "I see you've read about the new law," noticing the paper lying with his jacket on a chair.

"Yes I have," Brad answered.

"What do you think of it?"

"It's totally unconstitutional; it's a piece of trash," Brad answered.

"I can't see the Supreme Court ratifying it," stated Mary.

"Neither can I."

"There's one related thing that is bothering me though," Mary said.

"What's that?"

"I decided to read the article to my civics classes today and get some feedback. When I read the article to each period, the students seemed almost disinterested. When I asked for opinions, the general consensus was that we have to do whatever is necessary to stop terrorism. When I asked, even at the price of our civil rights? They said, 'That would never happen here.' I don't like their attitudes, and their attitudes reflect the attitudes of their parents. That's not good."

Brad agreed with Mary and added, "I sure will be interested in what your father will have to say about this when we see him on Thanksgiving."

"Oh, I bet he'll have plenty to say!" Mary stated.

After dinner, Brad got ready for his Thursday night class which started at 8 p.m. Soon he was out the door and heading for the college.

Alone now, Mary's thoughts drifted to the little retirement home her father and her mother had settled down in.

Her father had retired from his window cleaning business early because of a back injury. Fortunately, he had made some investments that afforded him a modest income for retirement. His country home was set on about five acres of land. He always loved space between himself and the neighbors. Sadly, her mother had passed away four years ago.

Mary was born six months before her father shipped out for Vietnam. He was in the Army Corps of Engineers. She used to listen to his war stories when she was old enough. Nothing gruesome, just the plight of the South Vietnamese people, and some funny stories about the guys in his outfit. After he came back from Nam, he was treated like a war criminal by most of the people he met, as were all Vietnam veterans. Although he never quite got over that; he never stopped loving his country. A short while later he watched as the civil rights revolution reached its peak. He couldn't believe that black people were treated the way they were in the south and other places in this country. He became an avid supporter of civil rights and studied the Constitution, especially the first ten amendments. Now, he loves to dabble in electronics, and build and fly radio-controlled model airplanes. Yes, her father is quite a guy, and she couldn't be more proud of him.

Mary decided to watch TV and fell asleep in her recliner. She awoke to the sound of the back door opening. It was Brad coming back from his class.

She said, "Hi, sweetie. How was your class?"

"Great, I learn something new every time I go. Oh, by the way, I aced my last exam, believe it or not."

"Now why wouldn't I believe it? I'm married to the smartest man in the country. We should do something this weekend to celebrate. How about a camping trip? We can go hiking and do some target shooting."

"Sounds great," Brad answered. "Why don't I see if Bill and Keesha want to come along?"

13

"Fine, but only if you guys promise to talk about more than just the latest electronic advancements," Mary warned.

"I think I'll call them right now and see if they want to go," Brad said enthusiastically.

"Uh, sweetie, they've been married just a little bit longer than us and it's 11:30 p.m. Don't you think you might interrupt something?"

"Like what?"

"Gee, do I have to spell it out for you?"

"Oh, I guess I'd better wait until tomorrow, huh?"

"Right."

Professor William J. Keats and his lovely wife, Keesha, were just about ready to sit down to breakfast when the phone rang.

Picking up the receiver, Bill Keats answered, "Hello?"

"Hey, Bill, it's Brad."

"Brad, what's happening?"

"Just called to see if you and Keesha would like to go camping for the weekend with Mary and me. We can do some hiking and target shooting."

"I don't know, Brad, let me see what Keesha has planned." After pressing the mute button on the receiver, Bill put Brad's question to Keesha.

Keesha said, "Why not? We haven't taken time off for fun in so long that I forgot what it feels like."

"OK, Brad, I guess we're up for it."

"Great, we'll be leaving at 6 a.m. Pack up tonight so Mary and I can pick you up at 6:05 a.m. sharp. We want to have as much time as possible at the lake."

Professor Keats kissed his wife goodbye and walked out the front door of his modest Cape Cod–style house. He drove to the university where he has been teaching advanced electronics engineering to graduate students for the past six years. He met Brad after one of his lectures. Brad had attended the lecture out of pure curiosity. After the lecture, Brad introduced himself and told Bill how much he enjoyed it. He had said that he didn't understand half of it, but still enjoyed it. Bill had laughed and they started talking. When they had found out they lived only a few houses from each other and enjoyed the same hobbies, a friendship had ensued.

Professor Keats opened the door to his classroom and walked to his desk. Most of his students were already in class and seated. Professor Keats put his briefcase on the floor beside his desk and stepped up to the small wood podium at the head of the class.

"Before we get started on today's lesson, I would like to pose a question to all of you. I assume all of you have either read or have heard about the ban on satellite receivers. Here's my question, is it possible for overseas TV transmissions to carry a hidden signal? Something that could be bounced off a satellite and then decoded by say, a special receiver? I want you all to research this and write a short paper about it. The paper will be due in two weeks. Now who solved yesterday's sine wave problem? Yes, Ann?"

After a hard day of teaching, Bill Keats finally pulled into his driveway and came to a stop short of his garage door. Bill had converted his garage into an electronics lab some time ago. Keesha had forbidden all that electronics junk from being in the house. So, the garage was the only alternative. He looked at the lawn as he walked to the front door. The grass looked a little high. He looked at the time; it was 4 p.m. He figured he had enough time to mow the lawn before getting ready for the camping trip tomorrow.

After the lawn was mowed, Bill started getting his camping gear out of mothballs.

"Thank God, I don't have to worry about a tent," he said, relieved.

Brad had a fold-out tent camper that slept eight people. Bill found his hiking boots, his wet-weather gear, cold-weather clothes, and warm-weather clothes.

"You never know what you might need camping in the fall. Geez! You'd think we were going away for a week," Bill said after surveying the pile of gear and clothes on the sofa..

He looked at his watch. It was now 7 p.m.

"I guess Keesha had to work over at the nursing home."

He was very proud of his wife. She had gone to night school and had graduated as a practical nurse, all on her own. Instead of working in a hospital, she elected to work at a local nursing home. She had said that she had always felt sorry for the elderly people in those homes, and that it felt so good to have the opportunity to help.

Just then, he heard a key in the front door and the door opened. Keesha came in with a tired smile on her face and said, "Hi, babe."

Bill answered, "Hi, sweetie. You look tired. Had to work over, huh?"

Keesha answered, "Yeah, we thought we had a runaway. Took us an hour to find him. We checked all around the outside of the building. Nurse's aides checked all the rooms. We finally found him hiding in the head nurse's office."

"Well, at least you guys found him."

Keesha had just noticed the piles of clothes on the sofa. "What's all this?"

"It's for the camping trip tomorrow."

"That's my Bill. You must have been a Boy Scout."

"What makes you say that?"

"You're always prepared for anything!"

They both laughed and went into the kitchen to fix supper.

Mary awoke to the sound of the clock radio playing "I Only Want to Be With You" on the oldies station. She reached over to Brad's side of the bed, but he wasn't there. The sound of the water running in the bathroom told her where he was.

She walked over to the closed bathroom door and said, "Morning, Brad." Brad returned the greeting. Mary said, "I hate to interrupt your primping time. Heaven knows you need it, but I've got to go!"

Brad opened the door and as Mary rushed past him, he asked, "What do you mean I need it?"

There was no answer forthcoming, just a giggle and the closing of the door in his face. Brad walked over to the full-length mirror and checked his look. "I'm still in as good of shape as I ever was. Well, close to it, anyway."

After breakfast, they threw their clothes and some foodstuffs in the camper and drove to Bill and Keesha's house. They were outside and ready to load their stuff into the camper. Upon seeing Bill's more than adequate supply of gear, Brad couldn't resist at least one comment.

"Bill do you know something I don't?"

Bill, realizing a satirical question when he heard one, said, "I just like to be prepared for the unexpected; that's all."

"Well I can't fault you for that."

The two-hour drive out to the lake was passed with small talk and much admiration for the fall colors. The ladies were in the back seat of Mary's SUV with Brad driving and Bill riding shotgun. Normally, if it were just Mary and Brad, they would have taken Brad's pickup; but with Bill and Keesha along, the SUV was more practical. Finally, they pulled into the entrance to the state campgrounds. They parked the SUV and went inside the ranger's office to pick out a campsite. Fortunately, the grounds weren't very busy; so, they were able to pick out a beautiful spot by the water.

By the time they got the camper set up, and all their gear put away and locked up, it was 10 a.m. They decided to pack a lunch, take a leisurely walk around the lake, and also explore the nature trails through the woods. The fall air was cool, but not cold. The orange, yellow, and red leaves were a kaleidoscope of color. The trees along the shoreline were reflected in the lake so that the color show was doubled. Each wooded path they explored was strewn with brightly colored leaves. Wherever the sunlight broke through the forest canopy, the leaves on the ground glowed brilliantly. Now and then, a stiff breeze would come up and leaves would be blown free of the limbs where they were attached. The leaves would fall all around them like a scene from a romantic fantasy movie. It made all four of them feel as alive as any four people could be.

It was 5 p.m. when they got back to the campsite. Brad and Bill got the firewood out of the back of the SUV and built a fire in the steel fire ring provided by the park. Mary and Keesha got the food together and brought it out to the fire. They put a pot of water on the grille over the fire with potatoes in it. There were ears of corn in aluminum foil to roast and veggie burgers for Brad and Mary. Bill and Keesha weren't so strict about their diet. It was hot dogs roasted on a stick for them. Darkness fell as they ate. They stoked the fire and relaxed with a hot cup of tea or coffee, and watched the fire slowly burn down. About 10 p.m., they decided to go to bed so that they could get up early the next day and head for the gun range.

The morning dawned sunny and bright. Everyone got up about the same time, and after making use of the indoor showers, they ate a cold breakfast of cereal and milk. About 9 a.m., they all piled into the SUV and headed to the range. The park ran the range and a ranger was the range master. They checked in with the ranger, picked their shooting positions, and waited for the command to check their targets. The range master gave the command "check your targets," and the four friends took their silhouette targets down range and hung them on the wire. They returned to their shooting positions and prepared their weapons to fire. Brad had a Colt Combat Commander forty-five-caliber semiautomatic pistol. Mary loaded her Glock nineteen compact-model nine-millimeter and waited for the command. Bill favored a smaller weapon than the hand cannons, as he called them, that Brad and Mary used. He was a devout James Bond fan. He loved his stainless-steel Walther PPK 380. Keesha was relatively new to target shooting and used a Colt Woodsman twenty-two-caliber target pistol.

The range master's voice over the loudspeaker asked, "Is there anyone down range? There was no answer, so he gave the command to fire. After a couple of hours of shooting, they ran out of ammunition, so they decided to head back to the campsite for lunch.

After lunch, the ladies decided to sit by the water's edge on the aluminum folding chairs they had brought and engage in some good old-fashioned girl talk. The guys decided to walk up the road to the ranger station so Brad could pick up a few brochures on other points of interest in the area. While they were walking, Brad asked Bill about the ban on satellite receivers and what he thought about it. Bill said that he didn't like it, and that his parents who went through the civil rights movement of the sixties and seventies didn't care for it either.

"Bill, is it possible for terrorist organizations to transmit secret orders hidden in TV signals?" Brad asked.

"You know I asked my class that very same question, and gave them two weeks to find out. There are ways to send signals across the whole bandwidth, but that would take very sophisticated equipment and decoders. I don't think terrorist cells would have access to such equipment, much less know how to use it. If you want my opinion, the answer is positively not."

"Let me ask you another question. Could it be a code of some kind?"

"Like what?" Bill asked.

"Oh I don't know. Maybe an Ottendorf Cipher for instance?" said Brad.

"How would that work?"

"Well, a listener could listen to a spoken sentence in say a news report and count the words. Every fifth word could be a key word in a sentence."

Bill pondered Brad's theory for a few minutes and answered, "There's a remote possibility but I doubt it. There's more than one writer for news stories and the same for dramas and soap operas. It would be too difficult to get the right word in the right place in a sentence. It would also be very difficult to keep track of the word count."

"That's exactly the same answer I came up with," Brad concurred.

"So what the hell is the DHS afraid of?" both men said almost simultaneously.

After the men left, Mary and Keesha talked about work, the fall fashions, what's happening on their favorite soap, and then turned to current events.

Mary said, "My students are very apathetic about the ban on satellite receivers and I wonder how you feel about it."

Keesha said, "I'm upset about it, because even from a layman's point of view; it violates the first amendment. I'm also alarmed at the lack of interest my co-workers have on the subject because they said, 'The government had to do what they had to do to keep us safe.' Then," Keesha said, "Bill explained to me that he believed it was ninety-five percent impossible for any secret message or signal to be transmitted by an overseas television station."

"So what the hell is the DHS afraid of?" both women said, almost simultaneously.

Chapter Two

Deputy Director of Homeland Security Hennery A. Hamilton looked into the mirror on the medicine cabinet in his bathroom. He had just finished shaving and rinsing the last remnant of shaving cream off of his face.

"Deputy director, huh?" he said under his breath. "Yeah, deputy director of the FBI, deputy director of the CIA, and now deputy director of the DHS. Always the bridesmaid, and never the bride! Well, that's all about to change in just a short while. My plan is in motion and that idiot of a president and the director of the DHS haven't got a clue as to what's going on."

He almost laughed out loud, but didn't want to wake his wife who was still sleeping. When he finished breakfast, he picked up his briefcase and went down the small hall to the garage entry door. He walked past his wife's minivan to the black, bulletproof Mercedes beyond. He pushed the button to disarm the alarm and simultaneously unlock the doors. He used the remote on the sun visor to open the garage door and then backed out of the garage. It was a forty-minute drive to the office building housing his section of the Department of Homeland Security.

When Hennery reached the underground parking garage, he showed his picture ID and his face to the guard who said after recognizing him, "Good morning, Deputy Director Hamilton."

He answered, "Good morning," and drove to his parking space. After parking his car and setting the alarm, Hennery took the elevator to the tenth floor where his offices were located. As he stepped out of the elevator, he was greeted with, "Good morning, Deputy Director Hamilton," from several of his employees. Each one, reminding him of his falling short of the position he had strived so hard to achieve. Even so, he acknowledged each one and went straight into his office.

He no sooner got seated than his secretary knocked on the door. "Come in, Stephanie." Stephanie was an attractive, curvy, tall brunette, very businesslike in her appearance, hair neatly done in a short cut, and dressed in a two-piece gray skirt suit.

"I have two messages for you, sir. The first is from the director; he wants you to call him immediately. The other is from your contact at the Supreme Court."

"Thank you, Stephanie. Oh, would you get me a cup of coffee please?"

"Yes, sir."

"Thank you."

After Stephanie brought him his coffee, he decided to call the director to see what his idiot boss wanted.

"Department of Homeland Security director's office," a feminine voice answered on the other end of the line.

"This is Deputy Director Hamilton; I would like to speak to the director please."

"Of course, sir. Hold just one second please."

"Hennery! Glad you could return my call so promptly."

"Well, after all, you are the boss, Jim." A fact Hennery hated to admit. *You're still an idiot, James Haggerty; no matter what you're the director of,* Hennery thought.

"Yeah, I guess I am, aren't I? I wanted to get your opinion on the up and coming Supreme Court case about the ban."

"According to my sources at the court, there's a fifty/fifty chance the satellite companies will be defeated," Hennery said encouragingly.

"That's not good. That's not good at all, Hennery! I stuck my neck out for you and this idea of yours, and so did the president!"

"Calm down, Jim. Things like this have a tendency to work out for the better good. I have a strong feeling that this happens to be one of those times. Besides, what's life without a little risk?"

"Maybe you think risk is fun, but it's my ass on the hot seat," Jim said. "We've spent millions of dollars" (*Closer to a billion, but you don't know it,* Hennery interjected in his thoughts) "on this project, and if the court kills it, heads will roll!"

"Jim, take a pill, get a drink or something, and calm down. In the first place, it wasn't taxpayers' money. You and the president both know that. In the second place, even if the court kills the bill, no one is going to find out about the money because there's no paper trail to follow! OK?"

"Well, since you put it that way, I do feel better. Are you and the wife coming to Nancy's engagement party this Saturday night?" asked Director Haggerty.

"Of course, wouldn't miss it for the world!"

"OK, see you then, Hennery. Goodbye."

"Goodbye Jim. Sheesh! What a worm! A little obstacle comes up and he's heading for the hills. He wouldn't have lasted fifteen minutes in the CIA."

Hennery took out his key chain, found the key for his bottom desk drawer, unlocked it, and pulled it open. He took out a file marked "The Dirty Dozen" and opened it. Inside were twelve handpicked operatives that he had chosen from his CIA days. These weren't your ordinary operatives. These were guys that, for one reason or another, were kicked out of the CIA. They were kicked out mostly for brutality or for too much collateral damage on a mission. Just the kind of men he needed from time to time. Using contacts in "The Company" as it was sometimes called, he had their records expunged, so he could put them on his payroll at the DHS In doing so, he earned their undying loyalty. Now, he had a mission for a couple of them.

"Yeah?"

"Dick?"

"Yeah."

"This is Hamilton."

"Oh! I'm sorry, sir; I didn't recognize your voice!"

"That's OK. Listen, I have a job for you."

"Whatever you say, sir." Hennery loved that kind of devotion; it was exhilarating.

"OK, now listen carefully. I want you to get Bob to help you and…"

After giving Dick his marching orders, Hennery remembered that his contact at the Supreme Court wanted him to call. His contact, Janet, was the secretary to the chief justice. He dialed her number and waited for an answer.

Janet answered, "Chief Justice Nelson's office."

"Hi, it's Roger," Hennery said.

"Roger" was a code name they used meaning: call me back on my cell phone. Since 9/11, all federal calls were monitored. Janet answered with, "I can't talk now," and hung up. This, of course, meant she could talk, and would call him shortly.

Hennery's cell phone rang, and he answered, "Hello."

"Hi. It's Janet."

"Hi, Janet. What have you got for me today?"

"I have some good news."

"Great, I could use some good news right about now."

"Yesterday, while I was at my desk, the chief justice was in his chambers with two other justices, and they were discussing your case. They left the door ajar, so I didn't have trouble hearing what they were saying. The chief justice said, 'Sometimes the amendments to the Constitution have to be bent in order to protect the common good.' One of the other justices said, 'Yes, bend, but not break.' The third justice said he didn't need much to persuade him that they were right."

"So what's your take on that?" Hennery asked.

"I don't think it would take much for the court to line up on your side. All they need is a push in the right direction!"

"I agree, and I think I've just put the wheels in motion to achieve that goal. Thanks, Janet. You'll find a generous envelope in the usual place."

"Always a pleasure to do business with you, Roger." They both laughed and hung up.

There was that face again, staring back at Hennery from the medicine cabinet mirror, the face of "Deputy" Director Hennery A. Hamilton of the DHS. It was Saturday night, and he and his wife were getting ready for the director's daughter's engagement party.

"You're not dressed yet?" Hennery's wife, Margaret, asked him. "We're going to be late if you don't get a move on!" she added.

"We'll be on time like always. Don't worry."

"I know you don't like these affairs, but I live for them. Besides, anyone who is anybody will be there. You might make some contacts to further your career. Maybe even get some help for that plan thingy of yours."

Hennery thought, *Right, "plan thingy"—way to stay on top of things, Margaret.* He almost forgot for a moment why he married such an airhead. Her father was a United States senator; seated on several powerful committees. It was the senator's influence that got the satellite ban pushed through so fast. The senator was the only reason Hennery was still married to Margaret. In fact, the senator was the only reason he had stayed faithful to Margaret all these years. He couldn't let a scandal ruin all his plans. Hennery wasn't just interested in being the director of the DHS; oh no, that was just a jumping-off point. A jump to the top, the presidency! President Hennery Alexander Hamilton, he liked the sound of that. Like his namesake, Hennery favored a strong federal government and an elastic interpretation of the Constitution.

"The rules have to be bent to keep the federal government strong and the people in line, uh, I mean safe."

"Hennery!" his wife's voice woke him out of his daydream.

"Oh, hold your pants on, I'm almost ready," he answered.

The baby-sitter had arrived twenty minutes earlier and was entertaining their two daughters in the living room. Just then, Hennery had a scary thought; someday he'd be having one of these shindigs for his daughters. *Well, not any time soon, they're only nine and eleven.*

They arrived at Director Haggerty's home right on time. Darla Haggerty greeted them at the door; Jim's wife was as bubbly as usual.

"Come in, you two. Wilma, take the Hamiltons' coats." Wilma, the maid, took their coats with a polite smile and trotted off with them. " Come into the great room and see who's here."

Darla Haggerty introduced them to the mother and father of the groom and some other dignitaries they didn't know. Then she turned Hennery and Margaret loose to fend for themselves.

There was only one guest Hennery was interested in, and he zeroed in on him immediately. It was William Taylor, the assistant attorney general, who was representing the government's side of the satellite case before the Supreme Court.

"Bill, how are you?" Hennery asked.

"Just fine, Hennery. How are you?"

"As well as can be expected. How are your preparations for the case coming along?"

"Oh, pretty good. I think we have a good chance of winning."

Hennery looked at the AAG and asked, "Could you use some more ammunition?"

"A lawyer can always use more ammunition in a case. You have any?"

"What if I told you that the DHS will reimburse all the satellite dish owners their original investment, and pay for their cable installation? We also will guarantee all satellite company employees will be hired by the cable companies to handle the huge increase in demand on their personnel?

"What? Can you do that?"

"You have my word on it."

"Then I think that will put us over the top."

Well, almost anyway, Hennery thought. He gave the AAG a big smile and handshake, and wandered off to see what kind of new contacts he could make at this fancy shindig.

As far as the rest of the party was concerned, Hennery could care less. There was a Catholic bishop who gave the blessing before dinner. Then, there were the usual chitchats during and after dinner. There was toast after toast to the happy couple. Then what's-his-name, the fiancé, and Nancy thanked everyone for coming as the party broke up. Couldn't happen soon enough for Hennery. Other than making a couple of new contacts, and his little talk with the AAG, the party was a bust for him.

Friday, October 29, 2021, found Hennery at work in his office as usual. Hennery was excited and a little nervous because he knew this Friday was going to be a special Friday. This Friday was going down in history as the turning point in the war on terrorism. There would be no turning back for him after today. This was the fail-safe point. He took care of a couple of reports he had been putting off, and did some dictation in his log for Stephanie to enter into the database. Before he realized it, it was noon, and time for lunch. Hennery ordered lunch in from the cafeteria. He wasn't going to take any chances on getting caught in traffic, and not making it back to his desk before 3 p.m.

After lunch, which took all of thirty minutes, Hennery turned on the TV, and tuned it to MSN. For the next hour and a half, he alternately watched the news and made some phone calls. Then, he looked over reports about last week's activities and actions taken by the DHS. Hennery looked at the clock. "Two-ten p.m.," he quietly said to himself. He had enough time to take some reading material and head for the restroom. He returned to his office twenty-five minutes later. Once again, he looked at the clock, and it read 2:35 p.m. Hennery said to himself, "It won't be long now."

Bob and Dick sat in their car in the parking lot off First Street, across from the oval plaza which is in front of the main entrance to the Supreme Court Building. They were dressed in suits with long trench coats over top, they were wearing hats, and they had brown skin makeup on their faces and hands. About twenty minutes earlier, they were in the Great Hall of the Supreme Court Building. They planted their charges precisely where Hennery had told them, and it wasn't easy either. There were tourists and security cameras to dodge, but they managed to place all nine charges in just under twenty minutes. Now it was five minutes to 3 p.m., and they were calmly watching the minutes count down to 3 p.m. In Bob's lap was a box with nine switches connected to nine miniature transmitters, all on separate frequencies. Each charge would be set off about a second apart for maximum shock value.

Shortly before 3 p.m., a family of tourists walked across the oval plaza, and up the steps to the front door of the Supreme Court Building. A mother and father with their two little girls walked through the open doorway. Bob and Dick watched the family walk through the doorway without a hint of concern on their faces. It was now thirty seconds to detonation; ten seconds; nine; eight; seven; six; five; four; three; two; one. Bob threw the first switch, then the second, and so forth, until all were thrown. The outside of the building looked exactly the same as it did moments ago, but the doorway looked unusually smoky. At about detonation plus thirty seconds, people were running from the building screaming and coughing, including the aforementioned family. Dick had started the car's motor before the charges were detonated. All he needed to do was put the shift lever in drive and slowly pull out of the parking lot. He turned right onto First Street and both men made a clean, orderly getaway.

About 3:10 p.m., the first report came by phone to Hennery's office. It was the ATF director's secretary doing her duty, notifying all department heads of an explosion or explosions at the Supreme Court Building. The director had already been notified. Hennery thanked her and asked her to keep him appraised of the situation.

Then, he stuck his head out of his office door and said, "I want all section chiefs in my office in fifteen minutes, no excuses!"

Hennery's meeting with his section chiefs went well. He gave them their marching orders, and put on an Academy Award performance.

He said, "Leave no stone unturned. Tell every informant that the usual payment is tripled for any valid info on the bombings," payments Hennery knew he'd never have to make! Later, Hennery placed a call to Jim Haggerty's office.

The phone rang three times and then, Jim answered, "Haggerty here."

"Jim? This is Hennery. I've been notified, and I have set the wheels in motion at my end."

"Good, I'm having a meeting in my office at 1700 hours; the heads of the FBI, CIA, ATF, and the NSA will be here. Of course I want you to be here too."

"Yes, sir," said Hennery.

Chapter Three

FBI Special Agent Daniel Crenshaw got out of his car at the scene of the bombings and made his way through the doorway of the Supreme Court Building. Crime scene investigators and ATF personnel were checking out the nine sites of the explosions. Special Agent Crenshaw looked at the damage in amazement and disbelief. There, before him, were the busts of the first nine Supreme Court justices with a hole blown into the middle of each of their foreheads. It would seem someone was sending a message to the nine Supreme Court justices currently seated on the court. Agent Crenshaw overheard two ATF agents talking about how it had to be terrorists protesting the satellite TV ban. If there's one thing Agent Crenshaw has learned in ten years in the FBI, it's not to jump to conclusions.

"Hey, Dan!" a familiar voice shouted. It was ATF Agent Josh Pittman. Dan and he had met in the Federal Terrorist Investigations School. After they graduated, they worked on several incidences together, from bombings to illegal explosives shipments.

"Hey, Josh. How's it going?" Dan asked.

"Great until about thirty minutes ago."

"Yeah, tell me about it. What's your take on this, Josh?"

"Someone went to great expense and risk to try to intimidate the court. That much is obvious, and the obvious choice is terrorists," stated Josh.

"You don't sound convinced," Dan observed.

"I'm not."

"Why not?"

"It just doesn't feel right. Too much precision, and too high tech for terrorists."

30

Dan said, "I get the same feeling."

"Nine different blast points. Did they go off simultaneously?" Dan asked.

"No. Witnesses said that they went off about a second apart."

"That means nine different micro-detonator receivers all on different frequencies."

Josh asked, "Receivers? Why do you think they were command detonated?"

"The charges had to be placed minutes before they were detonated or they would have been noticed even with the best camouflage. The timing would have been too close to set timers. Besides, I know very little about micro-detonators, but I'm sure of one thing; they can't possibly have programmable timers. How they were deployed, now that's a different story! If we can figure that out, we may get some real answers."

"Well, I do know one thing," Josh added, "you don't intimidate Supreme Court judges, no matter what you do. In fact, you might even get the exact opposite of what you wanted!"

"You got that right," Dan agreed. "Were the surveillance cameras working, Josh?"

"Yeah, the CSI guys are looking at the tapes now. Security was light though, almost non existent."

"Why?"

Josh answered, "Because court wasn't in session. There were just a few tourists, and they didn't see or notice anything. Tourism is light this time of year. There's one other question we have to think about though."

"What's that?" asked Dan.

"Why 3 p.m.? Why that time? Why not 2 p.m.; or 1 p.m.?"

"That's a good question, Josh; one that bears answering."

The press was all over the scene; they were outside, talking to witnesses, and trying to talk to law enforcement. Dan and Josh walked out onto the Oval Plaza and were immediately recognized by the members of the press. They were surrounded in seconds.

"Agent Crenshaw, were terrorists responsible for this attack?" asked a rather lovely woman shoving a Channel Six microphone in his face.

"We're not ruling out any possibilities at this point."

"But it most likely was terrorists, right?"

"We certainly will look into that possibility and others."

"What others, for instance?"

"We're keeping that classified for right now." Dan had no idea what others. He was hoping the perpetrators would see the report, get nervous, and slip up somehow.

"Agent Pittman, what's the ATF's take on this incident?" asked another reporter.

"I'm in agreement with Agent Crenshaw. It's too early to jump to conclusions and make hasty accusations."

Amidst a din of questions, the two men pushed their way through the crowd of reporters telling them, "No more questions, thank you." The reporters dispersed to start taping their lead ins for the six o'clock news. Dan and Josh promised to keep each other informed about the case, and departed to their respective vehicles.

Driving back to the office, Josh was puzzled about one question. "Why did the bombs go off at precisely 3 p.m.? Especially, since they were command detonated. That meant the perps waited until that precise time to detonate." Back in his office, Josh found a message from forensics to come to the lab to view the video from the Supreme Court Building. Entering the lab, Josh exchanged pleasantries with the head CSI, and then asked about the tape.

"We focused on the time frame from 2 p.m. through 4 p.m.. We figured anything before or after was irrelevant."

"Right, so what did you find out?" Josh asked.

"It's pretty uneventful until right here." He paused the tape where two dark-skinned males were standing before one of the busts, but behind the rope barrier. Both were wearing suits, dress shoes, hats, and a trench coat over top.

As the tape was started again, Josh watched the two men walk from one bust to the other, pausing briefly at each one. One of the men seemed to be more interested in his surroundings than the busts of the Supreme Court justices. The other seemed to be concentrating very closely on the busts and seemed to be doing something with his hands. Whatever he was doing couldn't be seen because of the trench coat.

"Send a copy of this to Special Agent Daniel Crenshaw, FBI. I want his take on this."

"Sure thing, Josh."

"Find anything out about the explosive yet?" Josh asked.

"Yes, it was a plastic explosive; probably C-four. Most likely set off with a micro-detonator. The C-four was tinted with an acrylic paint. Probably as camouflage to blend into the surface of the busts."

"How big are these micro-detonators?"

"Hard to say. I never saw one. I've only read about them. I've also seen a few schematics of them. Theoretically, with micro-circuitry they can be the size of two pinheads combined up to the size of a pea, depending on what you want to detonate."

"Theoretically?"

"Heck, no one even knew they existed until today,"

"Sounds pretty expensive to develop?" Josh inquired.

"Hey, Osama Bin Laden's got millions!"

"Yeah, I'm beginning to think this was terrorists."

"One other thing. We found trace amounts of petroleum jelly at the blast points."

"Petroleum jelly? Any ideas?"

"Not a clue."

"Include this info with the tape to Agent Crenshaw."

"You got it, Josh."

Josh got back to his office around 6:30 p.m. He sat behind his desk thinking about the evidence collected so far. The evidence did point to a terrorist act. That was obvious; maybe too obvious. Josh happened to look at his desk calendar, October 29, 2021. "Tomorrow is the thirtieth, the next day is the thirty-first, and Monday is the first." He wrote the dates down in succession. He looked at the two threes, and added them together equaling six.

Josh spoke out loud as he concentrated, "Another three and we'd have nine. Whoa, we do have another three! The time, 3 p.m. That makes nine. Two ones in the thirty-first and the first makes 9/11." The first of November will be the day that the Supreme Court will hear the satellite ban case. The obvious conclusion would be high-tech terrorists. Still, there was that lingering doubt, the cause of which he couldn't quite put his finger on.

Saturday morning found Special Agent Dan Crenshaw at his desk opening the package Josh had sent over. Most of the time, he was at his desk on Saturday, reviewing reports, or looking over evidence. Today was different though, the assistant attorney general was on his and Josh's cases. The AAG wanted answers, and he wanted them before court on Monday. Dan didn't have much of a life outside of the FBI, anyway. He was married once, but not for long. She couldn't take his extremely diverse working hours which were anywhere from eight to five, to twenty-four/seven. The interrupted vacations, and the cancelled days off didn't help either. He didn't blame her for ditching him. What woman wouldn't?

Opening the package, Dan took out the copy of the security tape and the report from the Alcohol Tobacco Firearms CSI team. He read the report and highlighted key points he thought were important. He then took a look at the security tape. He paid strict attention to the men in hats and trench coats. The two men were expert at hiding their faces from the cameras. A computer analysis and match of their faces would be impossible to make. They did look dark skinned like they were of Middle East origin. Dan looked at the report consisting of micro-detonators, C-four, and petroleum jelly. He kept going over these items, again and again. He watched the two men, especially the one concentrating on the busts.

"What was he doing? How did he deliver the charge from behind the rope barrier?"

Dan decided to take a break and see what was on TV. Sometimes, a distraction is a good thing. He turned on the tube and started to look through the on-screen guide. The guide showed movies, cartoons, cooking shows, home improvement, etc. Then, he checked the sports channels: basketball, football, a paintball tournament, auto racing, and sport fishing. Nothing seemed to pique his interest. He turned the TV off and looked at the list again. He noticed the notation at the bottom of the page were he had written it. The notation read "delivery method" with a question mark. All of a sudden, it hit him.

He lunged for the remote; turned on the TV, and brought up the guide. The answer was right there, and he hadn't seen it. Sometimes, he thought, he must be an idiot. He scrolled down to the sports channels, and there it was: "Paintball Tournament!" He pushed select on the remote, and there were four guys dogging around large box-type structures firing paintballs at each other. He took note of the weapons they were using. The paintball guns were a little too awkward and long barreled to hide under a trench coat in public. After a short search on Google, he found handgun versions were available with laser sight mountings. That was it, the final piece of the puzzle. The purpose of the petroleum jelly was to lubricate the C-four so it wouldn't stick in the barrel. They used as small an amount as possible on the sides of the projectile so the C-four would still stick to the target. Only tiny trace amounts would be left after detonation. A laser sight and a little practice would make hitting the target a piece of cake. Even though this was the last piece of the puzzle, it wasn't as significant as Dan had hoped. Paintball guns could be purchased at any sporting goods store, discount department store, and even online. Not even a little bit traceable.

Dan dialed Josh's office. "ATF Agent Pittman speaking."

"Hey, Josh. It's Dan."

"Dan, how's it going?"

"Great, I got the delivery method figured out!"

"Good, I got the 3 p.m. question figured out, also. Let's get together and compare notes. Maybe we can get a report out today to the AAG and salvage the rest of the weekend," Josh said hopefully.

"Do you want to meet here?" Dan asked.

"How about my building? The conference room is empty," offered Josh.

"Fine. I can be there in an hour."

"Good. See you then."

Because of the weekend traffic on the beltway, the drive to Josh's office took about forty minutes. He met Josh in his office and they took their evidence reports and personal findings to the conference room. Josh spoke first. He explained about the significance of the time, and the timing with the court date. He then gave his conclusion, "This was definitely a terrorist act."

Dan explained the delivery method, but had his reservations about it being a terrorist act. He asked Josh to keep it between them, but he thought the bombing smacked of the CIA!

"CIA!" Josh exclaimed. "What possible reason would the CIA have for defacing nine busts of the Supreme Court justices?"

"Well, you got me there, Josh. I don't know, but I do know that this was too high tech for terrorists. Micro-detonators? Come on! Hell, I thought they were just a rumor until yesterday!"

"Too high tech?" Josh asked. Do you remember the 1994 bombing of Philippine Airlines, flight 434, by Ramzi Yousef, the planner of the first World Trade Center bombing? It's even strongly believed that he planned the Oklahoma City bombing as well. Ramzi built the bomb on the first leg of the flight. A diluted nitroglycerine solution disguised in a contact lens cleaner bottle was the explosive and his electronic wristwatch was the timer and detonator. Ramzi wasn't as dedicated as the suicide bombers of today; he left the plane at Cebu. The bomb went off while the plane was waiting to taxi, killing one passenger and injuring others. I'd call Ramzi's plan pretty high tech, but it was just a practice run. He planned to bomb eleven airliners bound for the USA simultaneously, using the same method and the help of some accomplices!"

Dan answered, "Electronic watches for timers, detonators, and diluted nitro is not the same as C-four projectiles and micro-detonators. Anyway, terrorists like big bangs and lots of casualties, as you've shown by your examples. This bombing had neither. I think terrorists would have made a bigger statement."

"You don't call a hole in the foreheads of the justices' busts a big enough statement?" Josh asked alarmingly.

"No, and I think it was too complicated and subtle for terrorists. But, since I have no reasonable explanation for it being anything other than a terrorist plot, I guess I have to agree with you."

"Good! So our reports will agree?"

"Yep, point me to a computer and I'll type it up. We'll be home by 5 p.m."

"Now that's what I'm talkin' about," Josh said as he breathed a sigh of relief.

Driving back to his apartment, Dan still didn't agree with the terrorist theory. But there was something about Josh's insistence and the tone in his voice that made him go along with it for now. Dan had a gut feeling for lack of a better expression. He couldn't shake it. Josh knew more than he was telling. Dan felt that someone had gotten to Josh, probably sometime after yesterday's meeting at the bombing site, and coerced his decision. Dan knew Josh from their working together on other cases in the past. It would take a lot of pressure, from pretty high up, to make him close his mind to new theories. Dan wondered who could have changed his mind and why?

Chapter Four

Brad was driving to his next service call when his cell phone rang. He glanced at the dashboard clock as he reached for his phone. It was 3:30 p.m., October 29. Brad looked at the caller ID; it was Mary.

"Hi, sweetie. What's up?" he asked.

"Did you hear the news?"

"No, I'm between calls right now, and I don't have the radio on."

Mary said, "Someone bombed the Supreme Court Building in Washington!"

"Well, I'll be damned! Do they know who or why yet?"

"No, they're not saying; maybe terrorists, maybe not. They'll have more details on the six o'clock news tonight, I'm sure."

"Was there a lot of damage and casualties?" Brad asked.

"No, strangely enough, just some busts of some Supreme Court justices," Mary answered.

"That's weird. We'll have to catch the six o'clock news tonight and get some details. Well, I'm at my next stop, sweetie."

"OK. What time will you be home?" Mary asked.

"The usual, 5:30 p.m.."

"OK. Love ya."

"Love you too. Bye."

Mary arrived home later than usual because of a teachers' meeting after school. It was 4:30 p.m. when she started preparing dinner. She knew Brad would be home at 5:30 p.m., and she wanted supper ready by 5:45 p.m. They could watch the six o'clock news together while they ate. She was watching Doctor Phil, while preparing a chicken and vegetable soup, when the phone rang.

"Hello?"

" Mary, it's Keesha."

"Hi, Keesha."

"Did you hear the news?" Keesha asked.

"About the bombing? Yes."

"What do you think?"

Mary answered, "I don't know what to think. Brad and I are waiting to watch the six o'clock news to find out more details."

"Yes, that's what Bill and I are going to do, also. Bill just pulled in, so I guess we'll eat supper and watch the news. Maybe we can get together for coffee and a little shopping sometime this weekend?"

"That would be nice. As far as I know, we don't have any special plans other than yard work this weekend," Mary added.

Keesha ended with, "I'll give you a call on Saturday. Bye."

"OK, bye." Mary hung up the phone, put the pot on to simmer, and sat down at the kitchen table to finish watching Dr. Phil.

At 5:35 p.m., Brad pulled into the driveway and walked to the back door. It was November, and because of the time change from daylight savings time, it was dark already. The warm glow of the incandescent lights in the kitchen was a comforting sight. When he opened the kitchen door, the aroma of the chicken soup was a delightful tease to his appetite. What a fantastic feeling, to come home after a hard day's work out in the chilly fall air, and be greeted by a beautiful wife, great meal, and a warm house!

"Hi, sweetie."

"Hi, big guy. How was your day?"

"A little tough, but I survived. How about yours?"

"Not bad; had a meeting after school, and got home a little late."

"When I got back to the cable office, everyone was talking about the bombing. They all thought it was terrorists."

"Well, maybe the news will let us know tonight," Mary said.

They sat down to dinner at 6 p.m. and turned on the TV. The local news at 6 p.m. had a sketchy report about the bombing. So Mary and Brad waited to see what the national news at 6:30 p.m. had to say.

The bombing was the lead story for the national news. They opened with a reporter standing in front of the Supreme Court Building. The reporter explained what had happened, and then they went to the interviews.

"Hey!" said Brad, as he paused the live picture with the remote. "You see that guy!"

"Which one?" Mary asked.

"The one on the right. His name is Daniel Crenshaw."

"How do you know that?

"We were in the same Ranger company in the gulf. I kept the intelligence computers and surveillance electronics in good shape, and he was a special operative for army intelligence. We used to hang out together. I lost touch with him a couple of years after we got out. I wonder what he's doing there?"

"Well, if you would push play; we could find out," Mary suggested.

"Oh yeah," Brad said, pushing the play button.

The video started up again and Special Agent Crenshaw was introduced. The interview played and the report ended. Mary looked at Brad. He was sitting there quietly with a look of sadness on his face.

"What's the matter, sweetie, you look down?"

"I just saw someone I knew years ago, and he's a special agent for the FBI. Here I am, the same number of years later, and I'm just a cable guy."

"Hey! Don't you dare talk like that! You are a very talented and successful man. That big-shot FBI agent didn't bring you down in my eyes one little bit, and don't let it have any effect on you, either! You'll always be a hero in my book," Mary said admonishingly.

Brad looked at Mary and thanked her. "I needed that vote of confidence." Even so, there was a small gnawing feeling in the pit of his stomach. He knew that feeling would stay there until he made a bigger splash in life. Little did Brad know that the time would come sooner than anyone could know.

"So what do you think, Brad?" Mary asked after the news ended.

"I don't think it was terrorists. I learned a thing or two in the gulf war, and there are two things that terrorists like; large explosions with lots of casualties. This is too subtle and mamby pamby for them."

"So who do you think is responsible?"

"I don't have a clue. I don't have the info those guys have so I can't really say."

"Well enough of that. Let's go into the living room and just relax for the evening and watch some TV," Mary suggested.

Saturday was basically uneventful around the Spencer house. Keesha called Mary about 9 a.m., and asked, "Would you like to go shopping around 10 a.m.?"

Mary said, "OK," and the two of them left around 10:15 a.m. Brad and Bill were left to rake leaves on their own. Fortunately, Brad and Bill didn't have monster yards to rake, so they were done by 1 p.m. Just in time to get together, kick back with a beer, and watch some college football.

Sunday morning saw Brad and Mary dressed up and headed for church. They weren't what you would call regular churchgoers, but they believed in God and his salvation. So every now and then, they went to church to pay their respects to the Lord. They were accompanied by Keesha and Bill Keats, and, after church, went out to dinner. Even though Mary and Brad were into health food, they occasionally ate out. After dinner, they dropped Keesha and Bill off at their house, and went home to read the Sunday paper. That's when they found out about the official report on the bombings.

"So, it was terrorists after all," said Mary, after Brad read the article out loud to her.

"Well, that's what it says."

"You don't sound convinced."

"That's because I'm not. Micro-detonators, that's too sophisticated for terrorists. I don't believe it."

Monday, November 1, was cold and overcast as Brad went to work. He reported in, as always, and had an uneventful day. Tuesday, Wednesday, and Thursday were carbon copies of Monday. Thursday evening, Mary and Brad got the news of the Supreme Court decision, while watching the evening news. The decision wasn't much of a surprise.

The reporter stated that the high court validated the satellite receiver ban voting eight to one. The court, in its decision, stated that sometimes the Constitution must be loosely interpreted for the better good, and the safety of the people. The abstaining judge stated that the Constitution and the first ten amendments should be interpreted literally. The authors of these precious documents did not intend for these rules to be bent in the slightest. He also stated that the freedom of the press, right of expression, and the right to privacy are sacrosanct. He ended by saying that the decision made today is a direct violation of those beliefs. A quick network pole taken after the decision was released showed a whopping eighty-five percent for the decision, five percent against, and ten percent undecided. At 8 p.m. tonight, the president of the United States will address both houses of Congress and the nation. The president is expected to announce the next step in the government's war on terrorism.

"It was the bombing," Brad said, still looking at the TV screen. He was talking more to himself than to Mary.

"What do you mean?" asked Mary.

"The bombing did the exact opposite of what it was intended to do. The justices weren't intimidated, and they wanted to show it. Only one of them had the guts to say what was right."

"Yes, I see what you mean. We'll have to watch tonight, and listen to what the president has to say."

They watched an old episode of *Law and Order* from 7 p.m. to 8 p.m. Then, it was time for the president's address to congress and the American people.

The TV screen went blank for a split second, and then the familiar scene of both houses of Congress in session appeared. One of the national news reporters was trying to second-guess what the president was going to talk about. The reporter put his hand to the small earpiece in his right ear, and announced that the president was about to enter Congress. The scene changed to live, and the Speaker of the House announced, "Ladies and gentlemen, the president of the United States!"

The president made his entrance; saying hello to various members on the way to the podium. This president is one of the most, if not the most, charismatic presidents ever. He had won his second term carrying eighty-five percent of the popular vote. He is a handsome man; his appearance is impeccable: clean-shaven, with dark brown hair neatly trimmed, dark brown eyes, black suit, white shirt, and red, white and blue power tie. He is an extremely rare individual; one who commands respect the instant he enters a room. It's a sure thing, that many of the women watching were envious of the first lady.

The president began his speech, "Mr. Speaker, members of the Senate, members of the House, and my fellow Americans: today is a landmark day in American history. Today, we have dealt a blow against terrorism. The Supreme Court, in its impeccable wisdom, has validated a much-needed ban on satellite receivers. This decision dealt a blow to the terrorist communications network.

"I know many of you want to know what's next? First: I would like to address all the people who own satellite dishes and receivers. You have my word, as president of the United States, that each and every one of you will be reimbursed your original investment, down to the last penny."

A round of applause rose up from the members of Congress. No doubt, they were worried about their constituents being angry with them, and showing it at the polls.

"Second: the employees of all the satellite companies will be guaranteed jobs by the cable companies in their area."

There was another round of applause probably for the same reason as before.

"Thirdly, and most importantly, tonight, I am revealing a plan that has been secretly in the making for two years. This plan was negotiated with the cable television companies and the Department of Homeland Security. The plan has taken a year and a half of development for both the cable companies and the DHS. Now, I am proud to tell you that we are now ready to move forward with this plan. This plan will insure the safety of our citizens, and make our homeland more secure. Starting tomorrow, brand-new cable boxes will be delivered to every cable service in the United States. These boxes are unique because they have a feature that will help warn the citizens of this country of impending danger. This high-tech early-warning system is designed to warn the public whether the television set is turned on or not. A special electronic device in the cable box will automatically turn on the TV that the box is connected to, and give whatever warning is appropriate. Whether the danger comes from terrorists or natural disaster, the public will be warned immediately.

"The cable boxes also have an uninterruptible power supply which will power the unit for up to a month if the power should go out. The cable companies and the DHS will absorb the distribution costs of the boxes. Distribution will start on November 8, 2021, and hopefully conclude in the major cities on or about December 30, 2021. The rest of the country, such as suburbs and rural districts, should be completed by spring. In order to accomplish this goal, I have authorized the National Guard to provide technicians in each state to aid in the installation of the cable boxes. Our completion time schedule is based on the realistic figures of two hundred installers per 500,000 locations at eighteen installations per day. This calculates out to a completion sometime in early May 2022.

"The Department of Homeland Security will have complete control over the use of the early warning system, and will be responsible for any use of the system. Because of the secret nature of these boxes, and the highly sensitive electronics within them, a law has been placed before Congress. This law, I am told, is expected to pass within the next twenty-four hours. This law will state, among other things, that any tampering with, or disassembly of the cable box, is a federal offence. The offence will be punishable by a $100,000 fine, or ten years in jail, or both. This law is to protect the technology of the cable box, and to detour unscrupulous people from using this advanced technology in a criminal way. The law also provides that a television and cable box must be in every occupied structure in the United States. Every hotel room, motel room, rental property, warehouse, office, private residence, church, synagogue, and anywhere a space is occupied for any length of time will have a television set and cable box. We want to have maximum saturation to save as many lives as we can in the event of a national or local emergency.

"I would like to conclude by saying that this administration is steadfastly working to protect the citizens of our homeland, and will continue to do so far into the future. Thank you, and may God bless America." A round of applause roared as the senators, and congressmen and women rose to give the president a standing ovation.

"So, what do you think?" Mary asked.

"I'm not sure what to think," answered Brad. "As I have said before, he certainly is a different kind of politician. He's straightforward and to the point; no wonder he's such a popular president. As for the cable issue, it almost makes sense to me."

"Almost?"

"I don't know what it is, but I just can't get behind this thing one hundred percent."

"I know, I feel the same way," Mary concurred.

"The president does seem to put the people's safety first," Mary added.

"Oh, I think he's very sincere, and beyond reproach. It's the involvement of the DHS, and other agencies under their control, that I have a problem with."

"Well, you know those agencies, and the type of people in them, better than I do, Brad. If you're apprehensive of them, then so am I."

The remainder of the evening was spent watching TV until 11 p.m. Then, they decided to get ready for bed, and turned in about 11:30 p.m.

The next day was Friday. The only thing significant at work, for Brad, was the installation of the new servers for the early warning system. The servers were installed by government technicians, but wouldn't be powered up until the new cable boxes were installed. Saturday, Mary and Brad just sat around the house. Brad watched a college football game, and then studied for his electronics classes for the coming week. Mary did some cleanup in the kitchen, and decided to work some sudoko puzzles. About four o'clock, they decided to do some grocery shopping. Approximately two hours later, they returned home and put the groceries away. They ate supper and watched TV until bedtime.

Sunday was more of the same. After sleeping in, they ate breakfast and read the Sunday paper, while sipping cups of green tea. Around 1 p.m., Brad decided to watch a pro football game. After the game, they decided to go to the indoor shooting range and get in some target practice. They returned home about 7 p.m., ate supper, and whiled away the rest of the evening in front of the fireplace, talking about the possibility of starting a family. They both thought that their marriage was solid enough, and they were mature enough to start a family. They both realized a child would turn their lives around 180 degrees, but they considered themselves mature enough to handle it. Since the next day was a workday, they decide to turn in early.

Monday morning, November 8, dawned gloomy and early. It was starting to look like winter already. Brad got to work at his usual time of 8 a.m. In the bay, where the trucks were usually serviced, were metal folding chairs, and a lot of new people were seated in them. The new people were ex-satellite TV installers that the cable companies agreed to hire. The cable companies needed the extra help, if they were going to install all the boxes that the DHS wanted installed by spring. There was a folding table at the head of all the chairs, with one of the new cable boxes on it. Brad took a seat beside Jim Rathburn and waited for the briefing to start.

Tom Demarco, the personnel supervisor, walked into the bay area and over to the table at the head of the room. He started his lecture on the new cable boxes with a good morning to everyone.

"I'm sure that you old-timers have noticed that we have quite a few new faces here today. We're going to need these new guys if we are going to meet the deadline the DHS has given us for the installation of the new boxes. First, I have to inform you that the new federal law concerning these boxes was passed Saturday, in a special session. The law makes it a federal offence for anyone to disassemble or tamper with these boxes at any time. It is also illegal to relocate or disconnect these boxes after they have been installed. If service is terminated, or the customer moves out, the box stays in the house, apartment, place of business, or what have you. The only way a box leaves its assigned area is by removal by an authorized technician. There are also severe penalties, if we, the installers, lose track of even one of these boxes. So, you guys will be accountable for every box you sign out. If a box turns up missing, then the installer who lost the box is in big federal trouble. As for the customer, you are to give them a copy of the law and point out the warning label on the box. The customer is just as liable as we are for the box, and just as punishable. The customers can install the boxes themselves, which will make installations go faster for us. Punishment under this law is severe; ten years in a federal prison and $100,000 fine for each offence.

"Now, I'll explain installation and some of the features of this new cable box. Actually, installation is basically the same as the old boxes. Here you have your digital connections, HDMI connections, and also the standard cable in and TV out. There's one difference with this box. The television set plugs directly into this outlet in the back of the box. This is so the box can turn on the television, and turn up the volume to alert anyone within earshot of an impending emergency. Besides a built-in, uninterruptible power supply, the box has a built-in GPS locator. If the box is stolen or relocated, the GPS will give its location, even if the box is unplugged, and the authorities will be able to locate whoever is responsible. All the information about the law and the GPS is in the handout to the customer, and on the warning label. Even so, you should still point out this information and make sure the customer understands it. Customers who do their own installation will be informed of the law when they pick up their boxes.

"Because of the federal law, the brass decided you guys could only sign out six boxes at a time. That way the boxes will be much easier for you to keep track of; so don't say the execs don't look out for you."

"Horse pucky, they're worried about their own asses catching a federal beef," whispered Jim Rathburn to Brad. For once, Brad had to agree with Jim.

The guys upstairs could care less if we got nailed, Brad thought.

Tom asked, "OK, that's the end of the orientation. Are there any questions?" Someone asked about overtime. Tom said, "Anyone who wants it can have as much as they desire."

"That's what I'm talking about!" exclaimed Jim. Brad simply got up and went over to the office to pick up his work assignments for the day and sign out his first six cable boxes. He knew that there would be mandatory overtime also, and he wasn't looking forward to it.

The next fourteen workdays were hectic. Brad worked overtime, including Saturdays, just like everyone else. Only one thing wasn't like everyone else, he had to squeeze in his college classes, also. Then, November 24 rolled around; the day before Thanksgiving. Management let the installers off without overtime, and Brad went straight home. Mary had the food ready and their bags packed. All Brad had to do was take a shower and load Mary's SUV. Soon, they were on their way to her father's house. They'd been going there every year since Brad met Mary. Mary was tired from all the stress and work of making sure they didn't forget anything, so she decided to take a nap.

Brad looked at Mary sleeping on the front seat beside him, and thought about when they had met. Mary was one of Brad's first installation customers. They hit it off right away. *When the chemistry is right; it's right,* thought Brad. They dated for about six months and became very close. One November evening, they were relaxing and watching TV at Brad's apartment. Mary asked Brad if he would like to have Thanksgiving dinner at her parents' house. Brad's parents were killed in a traffic accident when he had turned eighteen. He lived with his uncle and aunt for a couple of years while working in their bakery business. After two years, he decided he just wasn't cut out to be a baker. He saw an add on TV one day about getting training in the Army on just about anything he wanted. He had always been interested in computers and electronics, so he decided to join. After six years and two tours of duty in the gulf, he decide not to re-enlist.

As a civilian, Brad tried to get jobs at various companies as a computer technician, but they wouldn't give much credence to his army training. So, he ended up taking a job at the cable company. Holidays were usually spent with friends, or back east with his aunt and uncle. When Mary invited him to her parents' house, he jumped at the chance. He was falling in love with Mary, and he hoped this meant she was falling for him. He met her parents on Thanksgiving morning seven years ago, almost to the day. Mary's mother and father greeted him like he was a long-lost son. Mary does have a brother, Donald, but he and his father don't see eye to eye on very many things. That first Thanksgiving, Brad felt like he got his parents back again. Mary's parents treated him like a son, and especially Mary's father, Paul Lorinsky. He and Brad saw eye to eye on just about everything, much to Donald's dismay. There was some friction between Brad and Donald because of it, but nothing really serious ever developed.

Two years after Brad met Mary's mother and father, tragedy struck. Mary's mother, Cynthia, died after a brief illness. Mary was devastated. She was very close to both of her parents, but especially close to her mother. Brad felt like he lost his mother all over again. It was one of the worst times of his life. The family gave each other support when they needed it, and everybody managed to pull through

OK. A few months after the death of Mary's mother, Brad proposed to Mary, and she accepted. Two years later, they were married. This will be the fourth Thanksgiving since Mary's mother died. Mary has insisted on making the turkey and side dishes every year. Donald's wife made all the fantastic desserts, and everyone usually had a great time. Brad was awakened from his daydream by Mary stirring awake and asking where they were.

"Almost there," Brad replied as he turned down the road to her father's house. They pulled into Mr. Lorinsky's driveway at 11:30 p.m. The front porch light was on, and so were the lights in the living room. They rang the doorbell. A six-foot, sixty-eight-year-old man, bald on top of his head, with gray hair and sideburns, brown eyes, glasses, and dressed in a plaid shirt and jeans answered the door.

"Hi, Dad," Mary and Brad said simultaneously.

"Hi, guys. Come on in!" Dad said, inviting them in.

Mary said, "Hold the door open so we can bring in the food."

After twenty minutes or so, the food was in and put away until morning.

Brad observed that Mr. Lorinsky had kept the house in the same condition and style as his wife had kept it. The furniture was early American throughout. There was knotty pine paneling in the living room, and beaded wainscoting in the dining room. The house was a two-story, turn-of-the-century farmhouse, over a hundred years old. Dad and Mary's mother, Cynthia, had worked hard to restore the house perfectly. The fireplace in the living room had a fire going in it, and it gave off a wonderfully warm glow. They all took seats in front of the fireplace.

"So how have you two been since I saw you last?" Dad asked.

Mary answered, "Just fine. I've been busy teaching school. Brad has had his hands full installing the new cable boxes, and will be until spring."

"You're still going to college aren't you, Brad?" Dad asked.

"Oh yeah, it's rough while I'm working overtime, but I'm not going to quit, that's for sure."

"I'm glad to hear it."

"So what have you been up to lately, Dad?" asked Mary.

"Well, since the model plane flying season ended, I've done some extensive research on the web, and started a blog on the Internet."

"What exactly is a blog? I mean I've heard the term, but I'm not sure I know exactly what it is," Mary asked.

Dad answered, "A blog is a journal kept on the Internet. I put information on it that I want to share with the world."

"Oh, I see, and what's your blog about?"

"Well, I've been concerned about the recent developments in Washington."

"That doesn't come as a surprise to us; we kind of figured you would have an opinion about it," Mary commented.

"I've done some digging, and I have put together a chain of events that are more than just disturbing. These events go clear back to October 24, 2001," Dad stated.

"That date is familiar, but I can't quite place it," Brad said.

"I know it. It's the date congress passed the Patriot Act, right, Dad?"

"That's my girl, the civics teacher! The passage of the Patriot Act was the beginning of a steady, but subtle erosion of our civil rights. I have accumulated documentation from newspapers, testimony before Congress, and information about the Patriot Act itself that will scare the hell out of you." Dad paused and glanced at the clock on the fireplace mantel and said, "Oh! Wow! Look at the time. You have to get up early and cook the bird; don't you, Mary? This discussion can wait until after dinner tomorrow."

"Yes I do. Thank you for reminding me, Dad." Brad and Mary said good night to Dad, and then went upstairs to Mary's old bedroom to retire for the night. Dad locked up the house just like he did every night. Then he went into the first-floor bedroom that he and Cynthia had shared for ten years. He sat down on the edge of the bed and slowly removed his work boots one at a time. Then he straightened up and tried to ignore the soreness in his lower back.

"It's not fun getting old," he softly said to himself. He finished undressing and went into the bathroom. He stood there in his underwear and looked in the mirror.

"Wow, getting old isn't pretty either!" After performing his nightly ritual of oral hygiene and the like, he put on his sleepwear and sat down on the edge of the bed once more. He thought back to when he and Cynthia had converted two small rooms on the first floor into a master bedroom and bath. It was quite a project, but with Cynthia's help and encouragement, they got it done. He sat on the edge of the bed in his pajamas and looked at Cynthia's picture on the nightstand. She had been very instrumental in helping him to forgive other people who treated him as a war criminal. She told him the public was just misinformed, and didn't understand who the returning veterans were. It was because of her influence that he got involved in the civil rights movement and became an avid supporter of the Bill of Rights. It had been four and a half years since she passed away, but on holidays it seemed like yesterday to him. He hung his head and said a prayer, then he kissed two of his fingers, and placed them on Cynthia's picture. He climbed into bed under the covers to lie on his back until he fell mercifully asleep.

Turkey day dawned rainy and cold. The morning was gray and gloomy with a snow and rain mix. The forecast wasn't very hopeful.

"Oh well, it's a great day for a fire," said Dad. "Come on, Brad, let's get some wood from outside and get a fire started." A few minutes later, a roaring fire was crackling in the fireplace. Brad asked Mary if he could give her any help in the kitchen, but she declined.

"She's just like her mother. Cynthia would never let me help on a holiday either. Ordinary days I could help all I wanted, but holidays were all hers."

Brad and Dad watched the Thanksgiving Day parade until it was over at noon. By then, the turkey and the freshly baked sweet potatoes and rolls had filled the house with their fantastic aroma. The doorbell rang, and Dad went to answer it. From his seat in the living room, Brad heard the combined voices of Mary's brother Donald, Donald's wife Anna, and their sons, David and Robert, saying "Happy Thanksgiving" to Dad.

After depositing the food they had brought with them in the kitchen, the boys and Donald entered the living room with Dad. Donald gave a cordial hello to Brad and took a seat in one of the easy chairs. The boys asked Grandpa if they could play a game on his Play Station four, and he said OK. They immediately ran upstairs to the bedroom that Dad used as an office and got started. Donald and Brad exchanged small talk about work. Donald was a police officer in a medium-sized city about three hours to the south. The only thing that Brad and Donald had in common was the fact that they started out in one profession only to find out that they liked another better. Donald had worked for his dad as a window cleaner for four years before deciding to be a police officer. Dad changed the channel on the TV, and the traditional Thanksgiving Day football game drew all three men's attention.

Mary was in the kitchen basting the turkey when her brother and his family arrived. When Donald and the boys left the kitchen, Anna stayed behind to put the desserts and ice cream in the fridge.

"Can I help with anything else?" Anna asked.

"Yes, you can help me set the table," Mary said.

While they were setting the table, Anna and Mary engaged in small talk. They talked about the boys and their schoolwork. Mary gave Anna some advice about how the boys could study for exams.

Then Anna said, "Donald's very upset about Dad criticizing the government."

"Oh, Donald would take the opposite opinion no matter what Dad thought."

"No, it's not like that this time. Do you know about the blog?"

"Yes, I found out about it last night."

"Well, Donald is convinced Dad is going to draw the attention of the NSA, or the DHS, and get into big trouble," Anna said with a hint of dread.

"Dad is exercising his first amendment rights and is under the protection of that amendment. I really don't think it's as serious as Donald thinks it is," Mary said reassuringly.

"Well, I hope you're right for everyone's sake."

"What do you mean?" Mary asked.

"Donald thinks Dad could get the whole family under suspicion."

"This isn't a police state. I think Donald is overreacting as usual. Now help me get the turkey out of the oven please," Mary said, ending the conversation.

"Mary and Anna, you outdid yourselves. That dinner was fantastic!" declared Dad. The rest of the clan agreed with Dad wholeheartedly. Mary and Anna cleared off the table. Then, they divided up the leftovers between Dad, Mary, and Anna's family, and started doing the dishes. Anna enlisted the help of her two boys who, under protest, reluctantly obliged. Dad, Brad, and Donald retired to the front room and took seats in front of the fire. Dad put a few more logs in the fireplace, and soon a roaring fire was crackling. Donald spoke first. He asked Dad if he was still going to put negative information about the government on his blog.

Dad answered, "I sure am."

"Dad, I know we haven't seen eye to eye in the past on several issues, but this is different," Donald said with caution in his voice.

"How so?"

"This time, you're going public with very inflammatory information. I think you might draw the attention of the wrong people."

"Like who?" Dad asked.

"Oh, I don't know, maybe the NSA, or the DHS?"

"Son, I appreciate your concern, but where would this country be if the founding fathers became fearful of drawing attention from the wrong people? This country was built on the concept of free speech, and the right to be secure in our homes and property. I feel that we are losing those rights, and I plan on showing as many people as I can why and how."

"Well, I think our leaders in Washington know best how to keep the people safe, and have our best interests at heart," Donald stated.

"You have a lot of company," Brad said. "The latest polls say eighty-five percent of the people agree with you."

"See, all those people can't be wrong could they?" Donald asked.

"Oh, it's happened before, and it very well could happen again," Dad answered.

"I give up! Just be careful, Dad, we all think the world of you."

After finishing with the cleanup, Mary, Anna, and the two boys entered the living room. Anna reminded Donald that they had a long drive ahead of them, and needed to get going. The next day, they were due at Anna's parents' house for a second Thanksgiving dinner. Pleasantries and goodbye hugs were exchanged all around, and everybody said they should get together more often. Then, Donald and his family were backing out of the driveway and heading down the road towards home.

Chapter Five

Mary, Brad, and Dad went back inside, after Donald and his family left, and took seats in front of the fireplace.

"So, let's see this information you've collected, Dad?" Mary asked.

"OK," Dad said. " I have to get the folder out of my office. I'll be right back."

Dad climbed the stairs to his office, found the folder, and was back in the living room very quickly. For sixty-eight, Dad could move like a man twenty years his junior.

"OK, let's see if I have everything in order." He checked the contents of the folder and gave a nod of approval. "We'll start with the Patriot Act. As you already know, the act was passed by Congress, October 24, 2001, but did you know that Congress approved it without most of its members even reading it?" Dad asked.

"What?" Brad and Mary asked astonishingly.

"It's true, copies weren't printed until after the act passed. At best, maybe, a handful of staffers actually read it before the vote."

"How could that happen?" asked Brad.

"Panic. It was only a few weeks after the September 11 attack on the World Trade Center. President Bush had declared war on terrorism, and pushed for more investigative powers for the federal authorities. Actually, the feds already had enough powers in place to do their job."

"What exactly, do you think is wrong with the Patriot Act, Dad?" Mary asked.

"Well, let me start at the beginning. You may already know some of this stuff, but bear with me. I think you'll learn something."

Dad began reading from his notes. "The Patriot Act basically gives extra investigative powers to intelligence officers, and other law enforcement personnel; both foreign and domestic. These powers include: monitoring and interception of email, warrantless searches where time is of the essence, increased surveillance, the ability to conduct phone and Internet taps with less judicial scrutiny, and the ability for the secretary of state to designate foreign groups as terrorist organizations and deport suspected terrorists."

Dad interjected here, "Now mind you, the secretary of state is appointed by the president and is not a judge or elected official. Yet, he or she has, under the Patriot Act, the ability to designate who is a terrorist, or what group is a terrorist organization, without any judicial scrutiny. The Patriot Act also allows law enforcement to detain terrorists who are not U.S. citizens for longer periods of time without a lawyer. Did either of you know that the FBI has used its Patriot Act powers against American citizens?"

"No I didn't," answered Mary. Brad frowned and shook his head no.

"According to the testimony of former senator Bob Barr, during a May 2004 congressional hearing against the act the senator said, 'The FBI has admitted using the Patriot Act for non-terrorism investigations, such as cases involving corruption in a Las Vegas strip club, drug trafficking, and other criminal activity.'

"Let me interject here," Dad said. "I know what you're thinking. So what, they were investigating criminal activities weren't they? That's true, but it shows that the FBI had abused the powers of the Patriot Act before it was barely two years old. The powers of the Patriot Act were created for one reason and one reason only: to fight terrorism and nothing else! According to the *Las Vegas Review-Journal*, the ACLU in reaction to this abuse of power stated that they have said from the beginning, 'That the Patriot Act included provisions that the government sought for years, that in no way had anything to do with the threat of terrorism, but could help them in your more garden-variety criminal prosecutions.' Other sources said, 'Because use of the Patriot Act in non-terrorism-related probes is controversial, local (Las Vegas) FBI investigators sought approval from the top echelons of the Justice Department before using it. Agents proceeded only after receiving express permission from FBI headquarters, and the office of the U.S. attorney in Washington D.C.'"

Dad interrupted his reading to say, "This proves that it wasn't just some local agents who took it upon themselves to use the Patriot Act powers, the abuse goes all the way to the top.

"The next obvious question is; why go to all the trouble of using the Patriot Act? According to the *Journal*, 'Law enforcement agents seeking financial records typically seek subpoenas through the U.S. attorney's office, and must submit evidence such as a sworn affidavit that establishes probable cause of a crime. The provisions of the Patriot Act require fewer elements of evidence to establish probable cause to obtain such records. Besides that lower threshold, a request made under the Patriot Act rather than a typical subpoena can yield a wider scope of documents.'

"'They wouldn't do it unless that was the only way they could get the information,' one source said."

Dad paused his reading to ask, "Do you see what they're saying here?"

"Yes," said Brad. "The FBI couldn't have made a case if it wasn't for the relaxed rules under the Patriot Act. I think I know what you're getting at. It's simple: the more they relax or expand the rules, the more they're abused."

"Exactly," said Dad.

"Now we come to Patriot Act II. Patriot Act II was written by the Justice Department to expand the Patriot Act powers. On May 22, 2004, testifying before the Senate Judiciary Subcommittee on Technology, Terrorism, and Homeland Security ACLU Legislative Council Timothy Edgar said, 'The advent of the Patriot Act II draft seemed to indicate Congress might soon be considering a major new expansion of federal power even before DOJ (Department of Justice) had explained how it is using the powers already granted, and before Congress had undertaken any substantial oversight of Patriot Act.'

"Fortunately, Congress was cool to the idea of Patriot Act II, so the Department of Justice and the supporters of the act did not go forward with the sequel," Dad explained.

"Attorney Edgar then goes on to say that, 'Supporters of Patriot Act II have continued to press forward with a strategy to satisfy a seemingly insatiable appetite for new and unnecessary powers without appropriate checks and balances. This Patriot II agenda includes separate legislation, and attempts to attach pieces of Patriot II to other bills.'

"Attorney Edgar was referring to the secret signing by President Bush of Patriot Act provisions slipped into the Intelligence Authorization Act on December 13, 2003. The Intelligence Authorization Act is an annual bill that generally gets drafted and passed quickly. These provisions gave the FBI the power to obtain the transaction records for patrons of libraries, internet service providers, telephone companies, casinos, travel agents, jewelers, car dealers, or other businesses without a court order. The FBI can simply draft a 'national security letter' stating records are needed for a national security investigation, without being specific about the data being sought, or the people being investigated, and without a judge's approval.

"The recipient of the letter is not allowed by law to tell anyone about the letter: not even the person being investigated. This means that some of the most private parts of our lives can be under investigation for any reason, and we wouldn't even have a clue that we were being investigated, nor could we do anything about it! Also the more the government is able to conduct its powers in secret; the more they can abuse those powers without our knowing it. As far as I could find out other bills with Patriot II provisions either died in committee, or never became law for one reason or another. I guess Congress wised up, but

I think the damage had already been done. Some people in the know said, 'That Patriot Act II became law on December 13, 2003.'

"So what do you think so far?" Dad asked.

Mary spoke first, "I think the government was chipping away at the fourth amendment, and pretending like it was still in place. Judging from current events I think they still are chipping away at it. They're trying to legalize illegal search and seizure."

Brad added, "I agree with Mary. I think there is more going on in secret than we can even imagine."

"Well, I think you're both right, and when you hear the rest of my findings you'll be more than convinced."

Dad continued the reading of his notes. "On August 1, 2004, the Bush administration and New York politicians told Americans that Wall Street was under imminent danger of a terrorist attack. Security levels went to orange, and then red. What the officials failed to mention was that the intelligence information was two to three years old!

"On June 10, 2004 air traffic controllers guided a plane near a memorial event for deceased president Ronald Reagan. The transponder on board the plane had failed just after takeoff. That's the device that tells the air traffic controllers where a plane is on radar, and more important, what plane it is. Well, the pilots did everything by the book, exactly as they should have. Only someone didn't tell the people on the ground about what was going on, so a panic ensued. The police told people that a plane was going to impact the memorial in seconds, and that they should run for their lives! Of course it was a false alarm, but the police had Supreme Court judges, members of Congress, and other dignitaries running for their lives! Was this an oversight, or was it deliberate? This incident occurred one week before the House Intelligence Committee was to consider expanding the Patriot Act. Also, during that week, portions of Patriot Act II were slipped into the Intelligence Authorization Act for fiscal year 2005. I think that was too much of a coincidence.

"On September 10, 2006, twenty-three men were arrested in England, and accused by the feds and British authorities of being bottle bombers. These men allegedly were part of a plot to blow up ten or twelve transcontinental airliners inbound to the United States. They would do this by using liquid explosives, and possibly killing thousands of innocent people. The feds had a few problems with making their case, such as the complete lack of evidence. None of the men had purchased airline tickets, and none had passports, which meant they weren't going anywhere soon, and no explosives were found anywhere in their possession. British authorities accused the Bush administration of political pandering. The actual scheme was uncovered eleven years before. It was the brainchild of Ramzi Yousef, the man responsible for planning the 1993 bombing of the World Trade Center, the 1994 bombing of Philippine Airlines flight 434 which was a trial run for the bottle bombing plan, and the 1995 bombing of the Murrah Federal building in Oklahoma City. The problem was, he had been in jail for planning these crimes for over a decade. By the way; the twenty-three suspects were released a few days later.

"What do you guys think the Bush administration was up to?" Dad asked.

"Sounds like fearmongering to me," said Mary.

Brad agreed and added, "Sounds like they wanted to keep the public fearful and aware of terrorists. Maybe to get more Patriot II provisions passed."

"You guys are as smart as you look! On March 6, 2006, President Bush signed the reauthorization of the Patriot Act."

"Son of a gun, they wanted to make sure that the time limit on the Patriot Act wouldn't run out!" Brad exclaimed.

"That was my conclusion also," Dad agreed and started reading again, "On November 2, 2005, President Bush admitted that the CIA was holding terrorist suspects in secret prisons abroad. Bush said, 'The United States never tortures suspects, but tough alternative interrogation methods are used.' He said, 'The CIA was holding key operatives involved in the September 11 attacks, the attack in 2000 on the destroyer USS *Cole* in Yemen, and the 1998 attacks on the U.S. embassies in Kenya and Tanzania.' The *Washington Post* reported in the same month that terrorist suspects were being held overseas not only at Guantanamo Bay, but in former Soviet satellites in Eastern Europe. The White House would not confirm the report."

"Wait a minute. Sorry to interrupt, Dad, but the administration's track record, from what you've showed us, isn't so good when identifying terrorists," Mary interrupted.

"That's right," Brad agreed. "They could have been holding and using alternative interrogation methods on innocent people! They could also have been holding them without the right to council or even letting their families know where they were!"

"Exactly my point!" Dad confirmed. Dad began again, "In the same statement Bush announced, that he was 'sending legislation to Congress that would authorize military tribunals for terrorist suspects.' The legislation also set clear rules to protect American military personnel from facing prosecution for war crimes. On June 6, 2006, the U.S. Supreme Court ruled military tribunals used in this manner were unconstitutional. They also ruled that Al Qaeda operatives were protected by the Geneva Conventions which ban 'humiliating and degrading treatment.' Bush called that mandate 'vague' believe it or not!

"Now, we have come up to the present, the year 2021. The Patriot Act is permanent law now with no expiration date. We still have secret prisons abroad. The last administration revised the military tribunals, so they passed judicial scrutiny. Because nothing ever happened in the case of the FBI using Patriot Act powers against Americans; they have continued to do so. There are also rumors that Patriot Act powers have been secretly expanded. There is reason to believe that there are secret CIA detention centers in the US; I have seen such reports on the Internet. I think it would be a small step for the CIA, FBI, or any other law enforcement agency to detain Americans suspected of terrorism; especially if they are of Arabic decent. You know that under the Patriot Act all law enforcement agencies are combined into one big agency so to speak?" asked Dad.

"Yes we do," answered Mary.

"All these agencies are under the head of the Department of Homeland Security. The director of the DHS is the most powerful law enforcement officer in the country, and quite possibly the world. When he says jump the only question asked is how high? He makes J. Edgar Hoover look like a Boy Scout! You know what they say about power don't you?" Dad asked.

"Yes, power corrupts, and absolute power corrupts absolutely," Brad answered.

"Do you think our current president is another President Bush, Dad?" Brad asked.

"He seems like a sincere honest man for a politician, but that's an oxymoron, so I can't really say. Actually the DHS has enough latitude to do a lot of things without the president's knowledge, or permission; nor do they need it."

"Well, the president certainly knew about the satellite TV ban; that's for sure," Mary said.

"That's very true. What about the bombing of the Supreme Court Building? Doesn't that sound like a Bush administration tactic—only much harsher? What do you think Brad,? You know about terrorists," asked Dad.

"As I told Mary the day it happened, it didn't look like the work of terrorists to me. Terrorists like big bangs and lots of casualties," Brad answered.

"I just remembered a question I wanted to ask you about Patriot Act, Dad."

"What question is that?"

"You said the Patriot Act was passed without being read, but didn't it have to go to committee before it went to a vote?" Mary asked.

"Yes, and it did go to a House committee. The committee held a lengthy debate with minority members succeeding in inserting several civil rights safe guards. However, the committee's work was summarily dismissed by congressional leaders, and replaced by a version of the legislation backed by the administration," Dad answered.

"President Bush established two important precedents for his successors." Dad started reading again, "One: the ability for the president and government to work in secrecy and circumvent some of the important checks and balances that our civil rights depend on. Two: invoking the president's constitutional authority to bypass a law. He explained it this way after he signed a bill on March 9, 2006. The bill required Justice Department officials to keep closer track of how the FBI uses the new powers, and in what type of situations. Under the law, the administration would have to provide the information to Congress by certain dates. Bush wrote a signing statement afterwards saying 'He did not consider himself bound to tell Congress how the Patriot Act powers were being used and that, despite the law's requirements, he could withhold the information if he decided that disclosure would impair foreign relations, national security, the deliberative process of the executive (president), or the performance of the executive's (president's) constitutional duties.' Bush wrote: 'The executive branch shall construe the provisions... That calls for furnishing information to entities outside the executive branch...in a manner consistent with the president's constitutional authority to supervise the unitary executive branch and to withhold information...' This statement was only one in a string of high-profile instances were Bush cited his constitutional authority to bypass a law," said Dad, ending his reading.

"So," Mary summarized, "what these two precedents are saying is the FBI and other agencies can do just about anything in secret, and the president doesn't have to report it to anyone, no matter what the law says!"

"Sounds like it to me," Dad concurred. "How about you, Brad?" Dad asked.

Brad was stunned. "Oh yes, I agree, I just can't get over the fact that the president can ignore law just about anytime he wants to. That's amazing!"

"I saved the best for last," Dad said, and then began reading. "According to the *Baltimore Sun* on August 5, 2007, President Bush signed a bill expanding the powers of spy agencies to carry out wiretap activities in the United States without a court warrant. The measure gives the National Security Agency and other agencies broader authority to monitor phone conversations, e-mail, and other private communications that are part of a foreign intelligence investigation. The administration said its intent is not to collect information on Americans. But critics said intelligence agencies are only required to delete Americans' private information from their records if it is deemed not relevant to the investigation.

"A congressional aide said, 'A little-noticed provision in the new law also suggests that warrantless physical searches of homes and businesses inside the United States may be allowed if the investigation concerns a foreign target of an intelligence investigation.'

"This law expired in six months, but the subsequent administration got it attached to a piece of rubber stamp legislation, and sneaked it through."

"How could they do that if Bush was caught doing the same thing?" Mary asked.

"Well, it seems the voters were disenchanted with Congress and voted in quite a few newcomers. The new congressmen and senators were inexperienced, and let the bill slip through. Even more remarkable is the fact that the two administrations after Bush were basically liberal, and civil rights conscious. That's how effective Bush's fear tactics were.

"So, starting back with the passage of the Patriot Act to the present day the federal government has been eating away at our civil rights, and we have been giving it our blessing in the name of fighting terrorism. I'm afraid the American people are in for a rude awakening some day soon. I don't know what kind of awakening, but I know it will be devastating. There are two things I do know though. One: once a government is allowed to operate in secret it will do so as much as it can. Two: at the present time the federal government has more authority and more unsupervised funding for law enforcement than any time in the history of the United States, and that's not a good thing. The more unsupervised authority and money they get, the more they think they can get away with," Dad said ending his statement.

Brad said, "Wow! Warrantless searches, wiretaps, military tribunals, secret prisons, suspects held indefinitely without counsel, president not accountable to the law, fearmongering; it sounds like the makings of a dictatorship, not a democracy!"

"It sure does, and it has me worried," Mary agreed.

"You should be worried, as we all should be. The latest polls favor the government and the president by eighty-five percent. I can't help but feel impending doom. I did find something peculiar in my research though," Dad added.

"What was that?" Brad asked.

"Well, after the Bush administration there were no bombings attributed to terrorists. There were a few bombings and bomb threats, but they were attributed to disgruntled employees and the like. Then starting ten years ago, two post offices were bombed; one in Baltimore, and the other in New York City, about a year apart. Then the terrorist threat was reborn so to speak. Four more bombings occurred. One at a federal court building in DC, and another in Boston. Then a federal reserve bank in New York, and another in Cleveland, all about a year apart."

"Yeah, I remember those. Not much damage and no injuries, except for mental trauma," Brad added.

"Exactly, it was as if the terrorists were using scare tactics, something they almost never do. Oh, there were some arrests made, and the so-called terrorists were tried before a military tribunal. The outcome of the trials have been kept secret because of the Patriot Act.

Then there is the more recent bombing of the Supreme Court Building along the same lines."

"Dad, are you saying it wasn't terrorists, but someone else wanting to make it look like terrorists?" Mary asked.

"It sounds farfetched, and I have no proof, but that's what I think. Who though? That's the question, and why? The bombings span two administrations. They started in the previous one, and continue in the present one. It just doesn't make any sense. What are they trying to gain?"

"That's a good question, Dad. I wish we had the answer."

"Dad, you should post your findings and observations on your blog as soon as possible, and please keep us informed about the reaction," Mary requested.

"Oh wow! Look at the time!" Dad said. The clock on the mantel chimed 3 a.m. "We better get to bed. Lucky you took a vacation day for tomorrow, Brad, because you'd never make it home tonight."

Brad agreed and they all said good night and went off to get ready for bed.

Brad and Mary slept in until 10 a.m. They went down to the kitchen for breakfast, or brunch, as it's called, about 11 a.m. Dad was up already, and typing away on his computer on line at his blog site. After brunch, Brad and Mary decided to dress up nice and warm and go for a walk. The rain-snow mix had stopped last night, and now the sky was partly cloudy with patches of brilliant blue. Every now and then the sun would break through and illuminate what was left of the fall colors on the trees. The air was cold. The thermometer on the porch post read twenty-eight degrees as Brad and Mary walked down the steps and headed for the field. The field had a mixture of tall grasses, raspberry bushes, and wild rose bushes. Brad and Mary made their way through the natural maze and walked into the wood line. They had been quiet until they reached the woods and found a path to follow.

Then Brad asked, "Remember the first time we took a walk together in this woods, sweetie?"

"You mean the first time you met my mother and father?"

"Yep. I was amazed at how easy it was to talk to both of them, and how well they both got along. It was by their example that I knew we'd have a good chance of being together for the rest of our lives."

"Well, it wasn't always like that," Mary said with disillusion in her voice.

"It wasn't?"

"Oh no, when I was seven years old, back when we lived in the city, my father was having financial problems. He and Mom would argue at least once a week. I remember one time in particular after they put Donald and me to bed in our upstairs bedrooms. They went into their bedroom and an argument ensued. My bedroom was next to theirs, and I could just make out their muffled words. I didn't know what was going on, but I knew it was a different kind of argument than the other times. My mother was alternately crying and angry and crying again. My father was asking her to forgive him, and that he loved her, and he would never do it again. Whatever 'it' was, I had no idea.

"It wasn't until I was eighteen and headed for college that I learned what that night was all about. My mother figured I was old enough to know the truth about all the arguments they'd had. Most of them were about money. My father was struggling with his window cleaning business because there was a recession going on and business was slow. She said they argued over almost everything imaginable, but the root was money. Well their love life suffered, and my father, sadly, had an affair."

"What!" said Brad, absolutely shocked.

"Yes, you heard me right, my father had an affair with a woman he did some work for. It wasn't much more than a fling, but my mother was devastated. She considered a divorce, but decided to give Dad another chance."

"She forgave him then?"

"Yes. She said she realized that she loved him, and he loved her, and that's all that mattered. Oh, they still had problems, but surviving that crisis made them closer and stronger to face them. I asked her why she told me about it. She said she wanted me to know that nobody is perfect. She was hoping this example would help mature me and sober me up to the realities of life. I was going away to college, and I needed to be aware of the fact that life wasn't always going to be fun and games. She said it was easy to get hurt, and she wanted me to be careful, and take college and my future seriously."

"Did it work?"

"Yes it did. Maybe too good, because I barely dated in college, and missed out on some fun parties, but Mom meant well so I don't blame her."

"Is that why you were kind of distant when we first started dating?"

" Yes, I knew you were the guy for me almost from the start, but I was still very cautious. After a while, I could see that your kindness and consideration were genuine. The rest is history."

"Why did you pick this point in time to tell me about this?" asked Brad.

"Well, we've decided to start a family, and a child can change a couple's life immensely."

"I know, and I think I've considered all the changes, but go ahead and tell me: maybe I missed one or two."

"A child is a huge responsibility, Brad. They need a lot of love; they take time, money, attention, understanding, and discipline. We both have to work to make ends meet. We'll need to hire baby-sitters, and buy all the things that children need. You know the number one reason for arguments in marriages is over money. We think it's a strain now to make the house payment, keep gas in our cars, and food on our table, but wait until after we have a child."

"I know the cost of living is high, but that's one of the reasons our current president got elected. That's why he's so popular, he's promised to straighten out the economy, and keep the country safe. So far he's been doing a pretty good job of both. The cost of living decreased this year by five percent, and he initiated this cable early-warning system. Besides, I'll finish college next year and get a higher-paying job anyway," Brad said encouragingly.

"I know, but it will still be a huge strain on our relationship, and I'm not sure it will hold up."

"Wait a minute. Are you concerned that what happened between your Mom and Dad will happen to us?"

"Well, the thought did cross my mind."

"I think if we ever get to that point, one of us should be able to recognize what's going on and defuse the situation before it gets out of hand. Let me get one thing straight with you: I love you, and I intend for us to be together forever. Besides, I'd have to be a fool to make the same mistake your Dad made, especially after learning about the terrible pain and sorrow it caused!"

"Thank you, Brad, that's exactly what I wanted to here."

"Good, now when are you going to quit using birth control?"

Mary looked at Brad, grinned, and said, "I already have."

She turned to run away, but Brad was faster and caught her.

He put his arms around her and said, "You little stinker, you knew all along what I would say, didn't you?"

"I had a good idea, but I needed to hear it from your lips."

"Well, my lips are about to kiss your lips. What do you think of that?"

"I think you talk too much."

He kissed her. It was one of those cold-weather kisses that warmed them from the top of their head to the tips of their toes. After a couple of minutes they came up for air.

"You don't have something to report to me do you?" Brad asked.

"No, not yet. It hasn't been that long since I stopped using birth control. We'll just have to keep trying. Think you're up to it?" asked Mary.

"Oh, I'm up to it all right. I'll keep trying every night until I get it right!"

"Every night! What have I gotten myself into?" They both laughed and started the long walk back to the house and supper.

After supper they sat by the fireplace with a crackling fire in it. Dad talked about some experiences he'd had in the Army, and in Vietnam.

"There was one time I remember," Dad began, "when we were in a convoy heading for a building site. The building site was a fire support base for an artillery battery to use. I was riding in the operator's seat of our twenty-ton truck-mounted crane, and old Fergy, short for Ferguson, the other operator was driving. We called him old Fergy because at the ripe old age of twenty-seven, he was six or more years older than most of us. We pulled out of Tai Nhin late in the afternoon. We were the last vehicle in the convoy, and I wasn't too crazy about that. About two hours into our trip, that took us through part of Cambodia, the truck engine started to miss and then died. I remember seeing the vehicle in front of us pulling away and leaving us. In those days a convoy didn't stop for anything, especially at dusk, which it was getting to be. Actually, I don't think anyone in front noticed we had stopped anyway. I never felt so lonely as I did at that moment. There was nothing but jungle and rice paddies on either side. If we stayed there very long we wouldn't be lonely much longer. I was sure glad Fergy had more knowledge of internal combustion engines than I did at the time. All the Army taught me was how to operate a crane, drive a truck, and perform maintenance on them, not repair them. Removing an engine panel in the cab, Fergy checked a few things and said the distributor had come loose. He turned the distributor with his hand while at the same time turning the engine over, and it fired up. I was never so happy to hear the sound of an engine running in my life. We caught up to the tail end of the convoy and made it to the building site. I shudder to think of what would have happened if Fergy hadn't been there. We were smack dab in the middle of Viet Cong and NVA territory, night was falling, and the night always belonged to Charlie."

Then Brad told a story about serving in the gulf.

"Do you remember seeing the FBI special agent named Dan Crenshaw on TV?" Brad asked Dad.

"Yes I do," answered Dad.

"We used to hang out together when we were off duty in the gulf."

"Really? He seemed like a pretty straight guy on TV," Dad commented.

"Oh, he is just that, and honest too. I'd trust him with my life. Well anyway, one evening, we were sitting in the officers club having a beer discussing a rumor that was going around. We had heard that Saddam had a cache of gold worth billions buried out in the desert. I told Dan that I had seen references to gold in the army databases. We were discussing how we could go about finding it, and how we would spend it, when the CIA section chief interrupted us. He was sitting at a table next to ours. He told us we were idiots to believe such a rumor, and the people who started it were bigger idiots. I think calling people idiots was a favorite pastime of his. We just kind of looked at him, considered the source, and thanked him for the reality check. You'd never guess the name of that section chief in a million years."

"What was it?" asked Mary and Dad almost simultaneously.

"None other than Hennery A. Hamilton."

"Who?" asked Mary.

Dad answered her question by saying, "The deputy director of the DHS, believe it or not; the second in command."

"You made that up!" accused Mary.

"Nope, did not," Brad denied.

Mary asked, "How come I never heard that story before?"

"I forgot all about it, but when I saw Dan on TV it brought back a lot of memories. Then last night when Dad was talking about the DHS, I noticed the list of officials he had compiled. That's when I saw Hamilton's name on the list of DHS officials. It was too late to tell you about it last night, so I waited until tonight."

"Do you think there was any truth to the rumor?" asked Dad.

"I didn't have top-secret clearance at the time, but I might as well could have. While running diagnostics on computers and servers, I could look up just about anything in any database the Army had. I found certain entries referring to a large cache of gold several times. Also, I found notes about members of Saddam's personal guards bargaining for their lives with the location of it. Three days after Dan and I met Hamilton, I was running a diagnostic on the army headquarters main server. I decided to try to find out the names of the guards who knew the location of the gold. I ran my usual search words: gold, cache, Saddam's guards, buried gold, secret cache, gold bars, anything to do with the subject. Believe it or not, I didn't get one single hit, not one! Someone had erased every mention of the gold and its location from every database in Iraq in just about three days."

"How could that be possible?" asked Dad.

"I can tell you how, but who, that's another matter. It was done with top-secret clearance, and a very special and powerful search engine. You'd also need a very fast almost super computer like the CIA had in Iraq to coordinate their operations all over the Middle East."

"Oh, so you think it was Hamilton," Mary guessed.

"It's a possibility, but if he got the gold what's he doing as deputy director of the DHS? He should be living high off the hog somewhere in Europe, or some exotic island somewhere," said Brad.

"Yeah, I guess you're right," Dad said. "Maybe you, Mary, and I can go to Iraq someday when things have cooled off, dig that gold up, buy an island in the South Pacific, and live like royalty."

"Not a bad idea. I'll take you up on that someday," agreed Brad.

Mary said, "I think you're both nuts!" They all had a good laugh and decided to end the evening on that note.

Saturday dawned sunny and cold. It had snowed lightly over night, and the morning sun made the snow glow a brilliant white. Brad and Mary decided to go Christmas shopping after breakfast. Dad decided to work on a couple of projects he had going in his woodworking shop in the basement. Brad and Mary drove to the mall located just on the outskirts of the city. They walked the length of the mall going in to each shop trying to get ideas for Christmas presents. They needed to buy for Dad, Donald and his family, Keesha and Bill, and a few others. They got quite a kick out of going into the "infants and toddlers" shop and looking at all the clothes and toys they would be buying in the future. The day went pretty fast, and before they knew it, it was dark outside. Before going home they decided to drive around and look at the Christmas lighting displays. They returned home about 7 p.m. with about half of their Christmas shopping done. That was a good start, because Christmas was still about a month away. After supper the three of them watched a movie that Brad and Mary had rented, and then decided to hit the sack.

Sunday morning was as bright and snowy as the previous day. Brad and Mary got up at 8 a.m. They dressed for church as they always did when they visited Dad on a weekend. They went downstairs, and immediately the aroma of pancakes and coffee hit their olfactory senses, making both their mouths water. Dad had been up for about an hour, and he had whipped up a batch of pancakes just like he used to when Mary was a little girl. They always had pancakes before church on Sunday mornings when she was growing up. The smells and the ambiance brought back a flood of good memories.

As they sat down at the table and started to eat breakfast Mary asked Dad, "Dad, why don't you have a dog?"

"Funny you should mention that, I was thinking about getting a dog only last week. You know after Big Dog died, when you were fifteen, your mother got a job to help out with the bills, and we didn't replace him. The reason being, nobody was home to let a dog out to relieve himself at noon. I never thought it was humane to make a dog wait ten or twelve hours to be taken out. We got Millie, the mutt, when we moved here, but unfortunately she developed cancer, and after only three years of having her, we had to put her down. After your mother passed away, I just wasn't in the mood to train a puppy until just recently."

"What kind of dog was Big Dog again?" Brad asked.

Mary answered, "He was a purebred bull mastiff, 120 pounds of solid muscle. That dog was a real character, wasn't he, Dad?"

"You got that right. We had a Siamese cat at the time named Barney, the same age as Big Dog. Those two would deliberately rattle each other's chain every so often."

"Like how?" asked Brad.

"Well, sometimes the cat would curl up on Big Dog's bed, but not to one side, right smack dab in the middle. When Big Dog wanted his bed back, he would stand there and whine, but all the cat would do is look at him and go back to sleep. So Big Dog was left with only one option, move the cat. So, first he would try to move him with his paw, but all that did was make the cat hiss at him. So finally Big Dog would get behind the cat, put his nose under the cat's body, and give him a flip with his head. This usually resulted in the cat flying about two feet in the air, and landing about six feet out from the bed. We used to laugh every time we watched that little scenario develop, especially when it ended. That cat never learned. He knew what was coming, but would never give in and just move off the bed."

"How about the time the cat got even?" asked Mary.

"Oh, that was a circus and a half! Big Dog was curled up on his bed. His bed was an old twin-sized mattress on the living room floor by the way. So he was curled up peacefully sleeping on his bed when Barney walked into the room. The cat walks over to Big Dog, sneaks onto the bed, and sniffs Big Dog's nose. He was probably hoping Big Dog was dead so he could have his bed. Well, Barney determined that Big Dog was still alive, so he just hauled off and punched Big Dog in the nose, three lightning-fast times, with his right paw. Big Dog jumped up, Barney took off running upstairs with Big Dog in hot pursuit. The rest of us were following behind Big Dog trying to get him to stop. We knew if Big Dog caught that cat he'd lose all nine of his lives real quick! Buy the time we caught up to them, Big Dog had Barney cornered under Mary's bed. Barney had picked that spot because he knew Big Dog couldn't fit under the bed. We got Big Dog calmed down and brought him back downstairs. In a little while Barney came down, and it was like the incident never occurred."

"Animals sure can be a lot of fun, but also a lot of responsibility too. That's why Mary and I don't have a dog, even though we'd love to have one. We just don't have the time right now to train, and take care of a dog. Maybe after I graduate, and get a better paying job; we can hire a dog walker for the times we aren't home to walk him."

"Anyone want any more pancakes?" asked Dad. The answer was a resounding no thanks.

"Well, we better get going then, or we'll be late for church." After clearing the table, they got their coats, went outside to Mary's SUV, and drove away to church.

The church was typical for the country. It was painted white with a tall steeple adorned with a gold cross. There were twelve concrete steps, and a handicap ramp leading to the large double doors in the front. In the sanctuary there were six stained-glass windows on either side. Brad pulled the SUV into the parking lot and parked next to a blue pickup truck. They walked up the twelve steps and through the large wooden doors. They were greeted by a nicely dressed elderly man who handed then a folded sheet of paper with the order of service printed on it. Dad said hello to several people he knew. Many of the people remembered Brad and Mary from times they had been there in the past. They found room for three in the third row of pews and sat down next to a nice-looking young couple and their little girl. The small choir entered and took their seats behind the pulpit. The choir director asked everyone to open their hymnals and turn to hymn number 147, "Oh What a Friend We Have in Jesus."

After singing a couple more hymns, and some spontaneous choruses, everyone took their seats. Announcements were made, prayer requests noted and prayed for, and the collection plates were passed. Then, Reverend Samuel Woodward stood up and took over the pulpit. Reverend Woodward was a slim, distinguished-looking man of sixty, with mostly gray hair, and a slight southern accent. He was clean-shaven, wore a very neat and clean navy blue suit, white shirt, and red tie.

He began his sermon by thanking God for the United States of America, where people have the right to assemble and worship the god of their choice. The statement was followed by several amens from the congregation. Reverend Woodward's sermon was from the book of Acts chapter nine. That's where Paul was chosen by God to be the apostle to fill the vacancy left by Judas. He said, "Paul had to be struck blind and then three days later healed to get it through his head that Jesus was who he said he was."

The reverend said, "Some people are still that stubborn today, while some people find it easy to believe in the Lord. It's all due to human nature and upbringing." He went on with his sermon for about another thirty-five minutes. At the end, Brad could have sworn the reverend was looking directly at him when he said something peculiar. "You know, God is always at work in our lives, and sometimes he has a special mission for us. That's why we should always be listening for his call to duty."

The service ended with an altar call and an additional hymn. Then everyone started to file out of the sanctuary shaking hands with Reverend Woodward and thanking him for his sermon. When it was Brad's turn to shake the reverend's hand, the reverend took Brad's hand in both of his, and wished him God's speed. Brad had never experienced anything like that before, but one thing was certain, he would never forget it. Back in the SUV and headed for Dad's house, they all talked about a variety of subjects, but Brad kept his little experience to himself. He figured he would relate the experience to Mary at a more opportune and private time.

They got back to Dad's house about 1:30 in the afternoon. It was cold outside, about twenty-three degrees with a stiff breeze blowing. The breeze added a wind chill factor of ten degrees. They wasted no time getting inside the back door where the warmth of the kitchen greeted them. Mary volunteered to make Sunday dinner.

Brad decided to be a comedian, and said, "Wait, don't tell me what you're fixing, let me use my psychic powers to determine that! Wait, it's coming to me, hold on just a little longer, yes! I can see it, it's turkey! Thank you! Thank you! I don't know how I do it! It's a gift!"

"OK, wise guy! Just for that you get to clean up the kitchen and do the dishes after dinner while Dad and I sit and talk."

"I saw that coming too! Am I amazing or what?"

" Get out of here!" said Mary as she threw a dishtowel at Brad's head.

After dinner Brad served his sentence in the kitchen while Dad and Mary went into the living room to talk and reminisce. Dad got out the old photo album, and they looked at pictures of Mom and Dad before either Mary or Donald was born. Dad said they were very young, and happy when they were first married. Even though they had their problems and arguments, he never stopped loving Cynthia, and he was sure she felt the same way about him.

"You really miss her, don't you, Dad?"

"Every day, and twice as much on holidays," Dad answered.

"Dad, why don't you come to our house this Christmas? We'll invite Donald and his family too. It might do you some good to get away for a while; besides, you haven't seen our house since we finished remodeling it."

"You know that sounds like a good idea. I'll come up a couple of days before Christmas and see the sights."

"That's great."

"What's great?" Brad asked as he entered the living room after finishing his kitchen duty.

"Dads agreed to come to our house for Christmas."

"That is great. I can't wait to show you our remodeling job."

Soon, always too soon, it was time to leave. Mary and Brad had to go to work on Monday, so they decided to leave while it was still daylight. They put their suitcases in the SUV, then said goodbye to Dad, Brad with a handshake and Mary with a hug and a kiss. Both of them didn't want to leave, but they knew they had too. Dad waved as they backed out of the driveway and drove off down the road. They had a great time as always, and were looking forward to many more holidays like it in the future.

It was 8 p.m. by the time Mary and Brad pulled into their driveway. It was a great holiday weekend, but they were glad to be home. They unloaded the SUV and unpacked their suitcases. Then Mary made both of them a hot chocolate. They both sat quietly together on the sofa in their living room, sipping their hot chocolate and enjoying the feeling of peace you can only get when you're home. After an hour or so they decided to go to bed. They had a busy week ahead of them and could use a good night's rest.

Chapter Six

"Hello?"

"Hi. Mary. It's Keesha. How are you?"

"Oh, hi, Keesha. Just fine; how are you?"

"Good, thank you. How was your Thanksgiving?"

"Great. Brad and I had a very good time, and yours?"

"We had a wonderful time. We got to see all of our relatives on both sides, and of course we ate too much. Mary, I was wondering if all of us could get together sometime this weekend at our house. It's been a while, and we miss you guys."

"Oh, I'm sorry, Brad has been so busy with the cable box installations and school that we've barely had time for ourselves. Brad is in Pittsburgh for a couple of days, and next week he is going to Boston to help with the installations there. He'll be back this Friday, and I'm sure he would like to spend a relaxing evening with you and Bill. How about Saturday evening?"

"Just what I had in mind, but only if Brad isn't too tired. You make sure it's OK with him, and if it isn't we will definitely understand."

"I'll ask him, but I'm sure it'll be OK. How does seven o'clock sound?"

"Just fine, we'll see you then."

"OK. Bye, Keesha."

"Bye, Mary."

Mary picked Brad up at the airport Friday night about 9:30 p.m. During the forty-five-minute drive home, Mary asked Brad about Saturday night, and he said it sounded like a good idea to him.

"I'll work on that paper I have to write for class tomorrow afternoon, and tomorrow night will be clear."

"Are you sure? You look tired, honey, and I don't want you to do something you don't want to do," Mary asked concernedly.

"Oh I'm OK. I slept on the plane, and I can sleep in tomorrow morning. I'll be bright eyed and bushy tailed by tomorrow night."

"It would be nice to see Bill and Keesha again. We haven't seen them for almost four weeks, and they only live down the street!"

After getting unpacked, Brad took a shower and hit the sack. Mary soon followed, and both were asleep in just a few minutes. No trying for a baby tonight, they were just too tired.

Mary was up and dressed at 8 a.m. She tiptoed down to the kitchen and made some oatmeal for breakfast. She served herself and put a serving for Brad in the fridge for when he woke up later. She looked out of the breakfast nook window at the newly fallen snow that covered the ground. The morning sun hit it at just the right angle to make it sparkle like tiny diamonds. As much as Mary loved summer sometimes she was grateful for winter. Winter was a restful time. No yard work to do, washing the car was all but futile, and gardening was out of the question. Oh, the holidays could get hectic, but they were over before you knew it. Yes, there was something to be said for winter all right. She was awakened from her thoughts by the sound of Brad flushing the toilet upstairs. She wondered if he was getting up now or going back to sleep. She listened to his footsteps cross the hall and head back into the bedroom. Then the creaking of the bed told her that he was getting back into bed. It was a game she played; seeing with her ears she called it. She used to lie in bed at night when she was a little girl and listen to her mother and father moving around the house. She would try and visualize what they were doing by the noises they were making. It was especially exciting at Christmastime when she could hear the sound of packages being placed under the Christmas tree. Mary finished her bowl of oatmeal with raisins, dried cherries, and dried blueberries. Then she read the morning paper while sipping her cup of green tea.

Mary looked up at the kitchen clock; it was 10 a.m.. The sound of Brad moving around again is what prompted her to look at the clock. Her ears told her that he had been shaving, and now he was finished and back in the bedroom. Let's see, ten minutes to get dressed, and another couple to get to the kitchen means she should heat up his oatmeal in about nine minutes. Brad reached the kitchen just as the bell on the microwave timer went off.

"How do you do that?" Brad asked.

"Do what?" asked Mary playing dumb.

"How do you time it so my oatmeal is done exactly when I step into the kitchen?"

"Well, you see, dear Brad, I truly am psychic. Not like you, who only pretends to be."

"Yeah right, you're not going to tell me, are you?"

"I'm going to let that be one of life's little mysteries for you, Brad my man."

"You're a pistol, must be why I love you so much," Brad said while giving her a kiss on the cheek.

Brad finished up writing the paper he needed for class on Monday around 5 p.m. He and Mary had supper about 5:30 p.m., and then they went to the bedroom to get dressed to go to the Keats' house. Mary took off her sweatshirt and jeans, and was looking through her closet for something to wear. Brad walked into the bedroom and saw Mary standing there in her bra and panties with her back turned to him. He couldn't resist going over to her and putting his arms around her. Of course she had heard him coming, wasn't the least bit startled, and enjoyed the embrace immensely. She turned around and looked up at him, he looked down at her and kissed her. I guess they were going to be a little late getting to the Keats' house.

"Hey, Brad and Mary, come on in," said Bill Keats as he welcomed them in.

"Sorry we're late, last-minute phone call," Brad said.

"Oh, that's all right; no need to apologize."

Brad and Mary went into the living room, and took a seat on the sofa. Keesha came in from the kitchen greeting them with a smile and a platter of all-natural cookies.

"Would you like some tea or coffee with those?" she asked.

"I'll take a cup of tea please," requested Mary.

"Me too," said Brad with a mouth full of cookie. Brad had an incurable sweet tooth and wasn't afraid to show it.

"So how was your Thanksgiving weekend?" asked Bill as his wife came in with four mugs on a tray: two of tea for Brad and Mary, and two of coffee for Bill and herself.

"It was great," said Mary. "We had a wonderful time with my dad, and my brother's family. We walked in the woods, went to church, and ate way too much."

"How was your father, and what is he up to these days?" asked Bill.

"Well, he started a blog."

"A blog?"

"What's it about?" asked Bill.

With Brad's help, Mary told them the story as best she could. After they were finished Bill and Keesha seemed shocked and amazed. Brad and Mary were taken aback by their reaction until Bill explained.

"You're not going to believe this, but my father bought a computer and took a course on how to surf the Internet. He was doing some research on Martin Luther King and the civil rights movement when he ran across a lot of the same info your father did. He's not happy with the work of the Bush administration either, and the two administrations after Bush didn't exactly win his seal of approval. He thinks the fear tactics are just a coverup so the federal government can gain more and more power. My dad feels the current administration has got something up their sleeve, but he isn't sure what it is.

"Dad said he marched on Washington with Dr. King to get civil rights for black people and minorities. Now those rights are being slowly eaten away in the name of public safety. He also said that fear is a great, if not the greatest political tool. People who are afraid will give up anything, or do anything to feel safe again.

"You know," Bill added, "you have to hand it to our fathers' generation, they diverted our nation from the path of oppression for minorities to the path of civil rights and freedom for all its citizens. They have a spirit, the same spirit the founders of this country had to stand up to those in authority, and to show them that oppression would not be tolerated in any way, shape, or form. Neither would they allow the abuse of any government agencies' powers. It's too bad that spirit has almost been extinguished now days in the name of national security, and the fear of terrorism."

"Bill, I think you're right," Brad agreed, "for the most part, but as long as there are people like you, Keesha, Mary, and me to keep that spirit alive by every means available to us, there's still hope for this country. We need to keep the American spirit alive as Americans, not Afro Americans or Italian Americans or Polish Americans or Irish Americans or any other people's ethnic origin. We need to unite as Americans under one flag with one language, or we will be divided and fall victim to an all-powerful federal government. A government that will rule over us with an iron hand with no regard for individual rights."

"How do we do our part, Brad?" asked Keesha.

"By exercising our right of free speech, and speaking out when we see injustice whenever we can. Always let elected officials know when we're displeased with what's going on. I don't trust the government anymore. We've lost too much in the name of keeping the people safe. I'd like to see all Americans adopt that attitude, so we can keep the American spirit alive and well."

"I can't agree with you more," said Bill.

Mary and Keesha were quick to agree also.

"I have a question for you guys," said Mary. "How many people do you think are talking about this subject tonight December 11, 2021, or on any other given night in the US?"

"Not enough; not nearly enough," Keesha, Bill, and Brad answered in turn.

"Therein lies the rub, dear friends; therein lies the rub."

The other three members of the foursome could only nod in agreement. Bill broke the moment of silence with a question. "Brad, I hear that you're working out of town. What's up with that?"

"The government decided that major cities should be covered first because they're key target areas for terrorism. Smaller cities like ours, the suburbs, and rural areas will be taken care of in that order. So, installers from less strategic areas are being sent to the large cities to expedite the installations and keep them on schedule. What it boils down to is that the new cable boxes and the new system will be completed by April as planned. As each city is completed it will go online so it doesn't have to wait for the protection of the system until April," Brad explained.

"What do you think of the new system, Brad?" asked Keesha.

"I don't know what to think. We already had an early-warning system in place, and actually, I didn't see anything wrong with it. The government says this system will be faster, more uniform, and under one authority. I guess only time will tell."

The rest of the evening was spent playing cards talking about Christmas, and how everybody was spending Christmas Eve. It was decided that they would all attend Christmas Eve church services together, and afterward go to Brad and Mary's for some eggnog and a gift exchange. Christmas Day would be spent with their respective families.

Chapter Seven

Nurse Keesha Keats sat at the nurse's station going over the paperwork associated with her job. She looked at the date on the desk calendar in front of her; it read Friday December 24, 2021, and the clock on the wall said 2:15 p.m.

Almost quitting time, she thought.

She still had some last-minute things to pick up at the grocery store on the way home from work. Then, home to shower and get ready to go to Christmas Eve services with Bill, Brad, Mary, and Mary's father. She was looking forward to meeting Mary's father; she had heard so much about him from Mary and Brad. It had been a busy day. There was a Christmas party for the residents. Then the usual meds rounds making sure everyone not only got their meds, but actually took them. Then there were mountains of paperwork to be done. At least no one went missing today, everyone was present and accounted for. Keesha was glad she had Christmas Day and the day after off. She and Bill were planning to go to Pittsburgh to see their respective families for Christmas.

Keesha finished her paperwork and once again looked at the clock; it said 2:50 p.m. She went over the events of the day, and patient concerns with Jenny, the afternoon turn nurse. Then she put on her coat, picked up her lunch bag, her book bag, and headed for the door. On the way out she saw Mrs. Cramer sitting in her wheelchair near the exit. Keesha asked her why she was there, and not in her room?

The thin, white-haired elderly lady looked up at Keesha, smiled and said, "Why, I'm waiting for my son and daughter-in-law and their children. It's Christmas Eve and I expect them any time now."

Keesha looked down at the frail woman and tried to hold back the tear forming in her left eye. If Mrs. Cramer's son and daughter-in-law showed up to see her, the walls would probably fall in. The last time they visited her was when they checked her in four years ago. It was Mrs. Cramer, and the many people like her, forgotten by their relatives, that moved Keesha to become a nurse and work in a nursing home. She told Mrs. Cramer that she should wait in her room because it was drafty by the door and she could catch a cold. Then she flagged down a passing nurse's aide and asked her to take Mrs. Cramer to her room.

Keesha walked through the front doors of the home and out into the chilly afternoon air. The snow was coming down in great big flakes making her feel like she was in a giant snow globe, or maybe a Currier and Ives painting. Keesha looked up into the cloudy skies and took in a deep breath of cold clean air. A few cold snowflakes landed on her face as she said a prayer, "Thank you, God for my loving husband, Bill, and please don't let me end up like Mrs. Cramer, alone and forgotten. You know, maybe you can do something about that. How about you hit her son up beside his head and get his butt down here to see her! I ask this in Jesus' name, amen."

Keesha walked over to her car and unlocked the door; she got into her car, started the engine, and pulled out of the parking lot. Keesha pulled into their driveway and came to a stop beside Bill's minivan. Bill picked up a pizza as a quick supper for the two of them. After supper they took their showers, dressed, loaded the presents and themselves into Bill's Town and Country and drove down the street to the Spencers'. Bill knocked on the front door, and Brad opened it almost immediately.

Bill and Keesha said simultaneously, "Merry Christmas!"

Which brought the immediate response from Brad of "Merry Christmas" right back at them. The presents were placed under the tree for later. Brad introduced Mary's father to Bill and Keesha, and in a few minutes they were all in Bill's minivan headed for church.

After the church service and during the ride home a discussion about the minister's sermon ensued.

"I had no idea that the phrase 'fear not' appeared twenty-eight times in the New Testament; did you guys?" Brad asked.

No was the general consensus.

"I find it amazing that so many people think Christianity is a weak and restrictive religion when the opposite is true," Mary commented.

"Yes, Christ came to set people free, not condemn them to a life of servitude and ritual. So many people get the wrong idea, it's uncanny. Christianity is a strong and powerful religion tempered with love for all mankind and womankind," Dad added.

"Fear is our worst enemy. It can take over our lives and bind us so that the thing we fear the most can walk all over us. According to the Bible the only thing we have to fear is fear itself!" Bill said.

"I like the quote Pastor Brainerd used, Isaiah 43:1: 'Fear not for I have redeemed thee I have called thee by thy name though art mine!'" Keesha said.

Everybody else said, "Amen to that."

"You know our talking about Christianity just reminded me about something I researched recently for my blog. I ran across an Associated Press article reporting that in Belgium on or about December 23, 2007, fourteen terrorist suspects were released because of lack of evidence. They were accused of planning the rescue of a convicted Al Qaeda terrorist. As in England in 2003 no evidence was found in a search of the fourteen suspects' homes. These men were probably arrested solely because they were labeled Islamic extremists, and that's the scary part. Even though these arrests happened in a foreign country, they could very easily happen here, and probably already have.

"There have been reports on the Internet about such cases over the years, but due to the secret military tribunals they can't be verified. Even the press has been taken out of the loop. Some people may say, 'So what, these are Islamic extremists, right?' My answer to them is, fundamental Christians, devout Jews or Buddhists or Jehovah's Witnesses or Christian Scientists or Seventh Day Adventist or any other religion could be called extreme, and could come under persecution out of fear or hate in the name of keeping the people safe."

Everybody agreed with Dad's findings, and wished there were some way to wake people up to the very real danger to the first amendment and their civil rights. People have to realize that fear can cause them to behave irrationally. Fear could cause Americans to lose their precious freedom to express opinions without persecution.

When they arrived at Brad and Mary's house they went inside, took off their coats, and found seats in the living room. Mary came in with eggnog for everyone and started handing out presents. Everyone opened his or her presents and everybody thanked everyone in turn. Soon they were singing Christmas carols, drinking eggnog, and eating some of Mary's all-natural frosted sugar cookies. Around 11 p.m., Keesha and Bill decided to head for home. They thanked Brad and Mary for a great time, told her father it was a pleasure meeting him, and took their leave. Brad and Mary watched their friends back out of the driveway and head down the street to their house.

Brad and Mary went back into their living room where Dad was sitting in a recliner chair.

"Well, Dad, Brad and I are heading for bed."

"Yes, I guess I will too. You have two fine friends there in Keesha and Bill. I really like and respect them."

"Thanks, Dad. We think they're great too."

"I probably don't say this enough, but I'm proud of you two. You've made quite a home and life for yourselves here, and I'm proud of you because of it."

"Well thank you, Dad. That means a lot coming from you," Mary said with gratitude.

Christmas morning dawned sunny and bright with a fresh dusting of snow on the ground. Mary was in the kitchen at 8 a.m. making the traditional pancakes and sausage breakfast. Donald had declined the invitation to visit today. He and his family were going to Anna's parents for Christmas dinner. He said that Dad could come to their house next year. Brad and Mary were a little insulted since Donald and Anna had never been to their house before, but decided not to let it spoil their holiday. They had a special surprise for Dad this morning, and they didn't want to be distracted in any way. Brad was already on his way to pick up Dad's special present. He would be back in about fifteen minutes. Dad came into the kitchen about 8:45 a.m.

"Brad still sleeping?" asked Dad.

"Uh no, he had to step out for a little while. He should be back in a few minutes."

"Where'd he go?"

"Well if you must know, he went to pick up your Christmas present."

"You mean I get something else besides that sweater you gave me last night?"

"Yes you do. Now eat your pancakes before they get cold."

While Dad was eating his breakfast he wondered what this gift could be, and why he didn't get it last night. Of course he didn't ask Mary about it. He didn't want to look like a little boy on Christmas morning even though that was the way he felt.

Just then they heard Brad's pickup pull into the driveway. Mary grabbed her coat, told Dad to remain seated, and not to peek as she ran out the door to greet Brad. She soon returned walking through the door in front of Brad, and blocking the view of whatever Brad was carrying. After they were both inside Mary slowly stepped aside, and Dad finally got to see his present. Dad tried unsuccessfully to hold back a tear that weld up in his right eye, and smiled ear to ear. Brad was holding a three-month-old bull mastiff puppy with a giant red bow around its neck.

"He was a rescue. We had the shelter owner hold him until today so we could surprise you with him. He's housebroken, neutered, has all his shots, and he's all yours: if you want him, that is?" asked Mary.

"Of course I want him," Dad said.

"Are you sure? We could always find him a good home. I don't think it would be much of a problem."

Dad walked over and took the puppy in his arms and said, "I don't think that will be even remotely necessary." The puppy started licking the side of Dad's face, and the bargain was sealed.

"What are you going to name him, Dad?" Brad asked.

"What else, Big Dog 2," Dad answered.

"Don't even know why I asked."

The rest of Christmas Day was spent taking care of the puppy. Making sure he didn't have any accidents, teaching him what was his and what wasn't, and letting him have his quiet time and rest.

Sunday morning, the day after Christmas, Dad was peacefully sleeping when he was suddenly woken up by a cold wet nose on his cheek. Big Dog needed to go outside. Dad got out of bed, put on his jeans, threw on a sweatshirt, his jacket, grabbed the leash, and escorted Big Dog to the back door and the yard beyond. After a few minutes the dog had relieved himself; a few seconds to clean up the lawn, and they were both back inside. Mary was in the kitchen just starting breakfast when Dad and his dog came through the door.

"He did everything a dog can do out there, so he should be good for a while," Dad reported to Mary.

Not being quite awake yet, Mary just nodded in approval. Dad went upstairs to see if the bathroom was available. Brad was still in bed so Dad took over the bathroom for a few minutes to shower and shave. After getting dressed, Dad went down to the kitchen for breakfast. Big Dog was lying on the kitchen floor gnawing on a chew toy.

"I fed him. Even though he was out we should take him out again in a few minutes," Mary said.

Dad said, "OK, I'll keep an eye on him while I eat breakfast." After breakfast Dad took Big Dog out again. Brad came down for breakfast and entered the kitchen just as the microwave timer went off. Mary took out the pancakes she re-heated for Brad and placed them in front of him.

" I'm going to figure that out someday; I really am," said Brad.

"You keep trying, big guy, maybe someday you will," Mary said encouragingly.

Mary went upstairs to shower and dress just as Dad came inside with Big Dog.

"Brad, I think I'm going to skip church this morning and just relax and bond with Big Dog. I'm going home tomorrow, and would like to relax and rest up before the drive home."

"You know that sounds like a good idea for all of us. I think Mary is probably exhausted from all the holiday activities and preparation, and could use a break too. I have to go back to work tomorrow, and from here on in it's going to be hell until we finish the installations."

Mary came downstairs, and Brad told her of the decision he and Dad had come to, and she wholeheartedly agreed.

Monday morning Brad left for work about 8 a.m. Dad packed his bags, ate breakfast, and loaded Big Dog into the pickup. After a heartfelt goodbye, Dad backed his pickup out of the driveway, tooted the horn, and waved back at Mary as he drove away. Mary was the lucky one; she was off until the first of the year. She didn't feel so lucky though. The house was empty, and she felt very lonely. She couldn't help thinking about something that had been bothering her for a while. She didn't say anything during the holidays because she didn't want to spoil the festive mood for Brad. Now that Christmas was over, she was going to talk to him about her concerns at the first opportunity, and she was hoping that opportunity would come tonight.

Brad got home about 8:30 p.m. all tired out and hungry. Mary had fixed something completely different, one of Brad's favorite meals, lasagna. After a shower and a change of clothes Brad entered the kitchen, saw the lasagna, and said, "Thank you, sweetie," and gave Mary a kiss on the cheek. "Oh, wait a minute. There isn't any turkey in that thing is there?"

"Of course not! Now sit down and eat."

After dinner they cleaned up the dishes and went into the living room. Mary sat down next to Brad on the couch.

"Brad, something has been bothering me."

"What is it, sweetie?"

"We've been trying to make a baby for over a month now with no results. I'm concerned that I may not be able to conceive."

"What!" Brad said. "That's ridiculous; you're in perfect health. You just had a checkup a few months ago."

"I know, but a lot can happen in a few months."

"What makes you so sure that you're the problem anyway?"

"What do you mean?"

"Heck, for all we know, I might be shooting blanks!"

"Gee, I never thought of that."

"I know, that's why I love you so much. You never point the finger at someone else until you clear yourself."

"Maybe we should both get a checkup, and find out which one of us is at fault?" Mary asked.

"I don't think there is anything wrong with either one of us. You know, some people think that conceiving a child is purely biological. I happen to think that there is a spiritual side to it also. I think we should keep trying, and when God thinks the timing is right we'll make a baby, don't you worry. Besides, I think it's a heck of a lot of fun trying, don't you?"

Mary laughed and agreed. Brad had quelled her concerns for now.

Chapter Eight

Hennery A. Hamilton, deputy director of the DHS, was getting ready for a New Year's Eve party at the White House. He was very happy Christmas was over and done with. Something about peace on earth, good will towards men, that just didn't sit well with him. Earlier this evening, 7:45 p.m. to be exact, he was in his study. He picked up his cell phone and placed a call.

"Hello."

"Bob?"

"Yes, sir."

"How's the baby doing?"

"The baby is just fine. She's sleeping in her cradle."

"You'll make the call at the proper time then?"

"Yes, sir."

"Good," Hennery said hanging up the phone.

Hennery sat in his home office, and waited for the call from Boston. At 8:05 p.m. the call came in from the Boston office of the NSA. The agent informed him that they had received a bomb tip. The bomb was set to go off 10:15 p.m. Hennery played dumb and asked where the bomb was. The agent informed him that it was Copley Square, and that a New Year's Eve concert was scheduled to start in two hours. The concert would draw hundreds if not thousands of people. Hotels that were full of patrons for the holidays also surrounded the square. It would take over two hours just to notify all the people in the hotels.

Hennery said, "Listen carefully. Send bomb search teams with dogs to the square, and personnel to evacuate the square of concert early birds. Inform the police to cordon off a five-block radius around the square. I am authorizing you to activate the early-warning system for Boston. Announce that the concert is cancelled because of a terrorist threat, and everybody should stay away from Copley Square until further notice. Tell the people in the hotels, via the system, to stay inside until the all clear is given."

"Do you think activating the system is necessary? It's just a tip," asked the voice on the other end of the line.

"Are you prepared to let a thousand people die, because you think this might be a gag?"

"No, sir."

"Then I suggest you get your ass in gear and follow my orders. Also keep me informed as to what you find out. Got it?"

"Yes, sir!"

Geez, what an idiot! Hennery thought.

Hennery leaned back in his desk chair and smiled. He looked at the desk clock Margaret had given him for Christmas last year; it said 8:15 p.m. By now the system was warning all the little citizens of Boston, Massachusetts, of the terrorist threat. In about an hour or so the search teams will find the bomb. Then they'll find out that they can't defuse it, or even move it without detonating it. Hell, they can't even touch the damn thing without it going off. They'll have to contain the device the best way they can and wait for detonation or detonate it themselves. Either way the New Year would start with a bigger bang than anyone expected, and he would be the hero of the day. He called his boss and informed him of the crisis and as always, Haggerty told him he trusted his judgment. Haggerty said he would inform the president so he wouldn't get blindsided by the press.

Hennery's wife had been flitting around all day getting ready for this event, and now she was nervously putting the finishing touches on her makeup.

"Are you ready, dear?" she asked, bringing him out of his little flashback.

"I'm as ready as I will ever be," Hennery said, as he stepped out of the dressing room that adjoined the master bedroom. "You look beautiful as always, my dear."

Margaret turned and looked at him as though a stranger had walked into the room.

"Thank you, I think. You must be in a good mood tonight to compliment me so highly, and with so much sincerity."

Hennery walked over to his wife of fifteen years and looked her in the eyes.

"I am in a good mood, but that's not why I complimented you. I truly think you look beautiful tonight."

"Well in that case, I apologize for my skepticism, and accept your compliment in the manner with which it was intended."

She punctuated her statement with a kiss to Hennery's right cheek.

"Mom, Dad, the limo is here!" shouted their oldest daughter from downstairs.

"OK, we'll be right down!" shouted Margaret.

They both headed downstairs. When they reached the bottom of the stairs, their daughters were full of ooh's and ah's over the way they looked. Margaret gave the sitter last-minute instructions, and told her two daughters to behave for the sitter. She also instructed them to go to bed after the midnight countdown. The chauffeur was waiting by the rear door of the limo. As they approached, he opened the door and Margaret got in, then he trotted over to the other side and let Hennery in.

The twenty minutes or so it took to drive to the White House were spent discussing the past year, and who would be at the party. Their limo pulled into the circular driveway that led to the front portico of the White House at precisely ten minutes to 10 p.m. They were third in line to unload so it gave Hennery a moment or two to fantasize. Someday he would be receiving guests here himself as president. Then it was their turn to unload. The chauffeur got out, trotted around to the passenger side rear, and opened the door for Margaret;

Hennery just slid out behind her. Margaret took Hennery's arm as they started up the stairs, between the massive white pillars, leading to the front door of the White House.

They walked through the front door into the magnificent entrance hall with its checkerboard gray-and-tan marble floor, and the red carpet beyond. A Secret Service agent checked their invitation. Then he ran a handheld metal detector over their bodies, and cleared them on. A White House staff member dressed in appropriate formal black-and-white attire took their coats and handed them a numbered ticket. They were directed to their left, to the East Room of the White House, where most notable events are held.

As they walked into the room another White House staff member took their invitation and announced their arrival. " Mr. Hennery A. Hamilton, deputy director of Homeland Security, and Mrs. Hamilton!" he said.

Hennery was pleasantly surprised to see a good number of faces turn to look, and wave hello. He hadn't realized they were so well known.

There were a total of six large Christmas trees in the room, and each one glowed with over a thousand white lights. The ornaments were burgundy and gold with burgundy-and-gold garland. The decorated trees were breathtaking, and so was the forty-foot table with every kind of hors d'oeuvre imaginable. The table was covered with a burgundy satin tablecloth. A pine bough garland adorned the table edge in scallops with white twinkle lights intertwined. Gold satin bows were attached in between each scallop. A huge champagne punch fountain adorned the center of the table. Kitchen staff scurried in and out replenishing the hors d'oeuvres. Servers wandered throughout the room with champagne glasses full of punch for the guests. In another corner of the room a string quartet was playing classical music. Hennery spied his boss James Haggerty and his wife Darla. They were conversing with the FBI director, the secretary of state, and their respective wives beside the large fireplace near the portrait of George Washington. The fireplace mantel was beautifully adorned with pine boughs, white twinkle lights, and large burgundy-and-gold hand-blown glass balls.

Hennery took Margaret's hand and walked over to his boss. James, seeing Hennery approach said, "Happy New Year, Hennery! Margaret, you look gorgeous! Let me introduce you. You of course know John McGuire, director of the FBI, and his lovely wife Scarlet." Handshakes and compliments were briefly exchanged.

"I would also like to present Secretary of State Jackson Mosscovich and his lovely wife Cynthia. This is my second in command, Hennery Hamilton, and his wife Margaret."

Hennery winced a little at being called second in command, but shrugged it off. Again handshakes and pleasantries were exchanged. Just then the sound of the guests' voices, as they engaged in conversation, were silenced by the words, "Ladies and gentlemen, may I present the president of the United States, and the first lady!" The string quartet began playing "Hail to the Chief," and all heads turned to look at the presidential couple as they entered the room.

The president was wearing a black tuxedo with a red bow tie, white shirt, and red cummerbund. The first lady was wearing a beautiful white silk gown with red accessories. At forty-five and forty-two years old respectively, they looked like the most perfect couple that ever walked the earth, much less occupied the White House. The only presidential couple that could hold a candle to them was President John Kennedy, and first lady Jacquelyn back in the early 1960s. Amidst a round of applause, the president and first lady made their way around the room paying their respects to each guest in turn. When they got to Hennery's little group, the president surprised the hell out of Hennery by calling him by his first name. Hennery's ego got a boost that it didn't need.

Hennery thought to himself, *This is going to be a very rewarding night; a very rewarding night indeed.*

K-9 Explosives Search Team call number 126 was waiting at the perimeter of Copley Square in Boston for the go-ahead to search. About one hundred yards away was K-9 EST 134, waiting for the same order. It was 9 p.m. It took almost forty-five minutes to clear out the early birds and secure the five-block radius around the square. Thanks to the EWS about ninety-five percent of the hotel patrons were notified, and were holed up in their rooms. Guards had been posted in the hotel lobbies to stop anyone not informed of the situation from walking out into the streets. EST 126 looked at the rows and rows of chairs that were between him and the stage. He knew that they wouldn't have time, even with dogs, to search them all.

"One twenty-six to one thirty-four."

"Go ahead," came the response from 134.

"I got a hunch this bomb isn't the size of a bread box."

"I was thinking the same thing; too many soft targets. They'd be looking to take out as many targets as possible," 134 reasoned.

"Exactly what I was thinking; I guess great minds work alike. How about we start at the stage and work our way out?" proposed 126.

"Good idea. We'll take the first ten rows, and you guys take the stage."

"Roger that," 126 confirmed.

"Cleared to search," came the command over the radio. Both EST. units moved forward. EST 134 stopped at the tenth row, and started a systematic search of each row. EST 126 went straight to the stage were the band's equipment had been placed earlier. Starting his search at the right-hand edge of the stage, it didn't take long for the dog to hit on explosives. Unfortunately, they were the pyrotechnics for the band's performance. Continuing the search in a semicircle the dog hit on a speaker sitting about mid-stage.

"One twenty-six to one thirty-four."

"Go."

"We've got something here. I need you to confirm."

"On my way." EST 134 came up on the stage and immediately his dog hit on the speaker.

"One twenty-six to five o five."

"Five o five go ahead."

"We have your package on the stage. Marking with orange dye now."

"Good work, you guys. Thank the dogs, and give them an extra biscuit on me."

"Will do. One twenty-six out."

EST 505 and his team headed for the stage. Dressed in heavy bomb squad armor, they approached the speaker with the big orange "B" on its front. Normally they wouldn't get this close this early, but the search teams were just there, and they knew it was safe. They placed a portable x-ray unit in front of the bomb and turned it on. They could hardly believe their eyes. The bomb was in essence a huge Claymore mine. At least one hundred pounds of home made plastic explosives configured in a shape charge facing the audience. In front of the charge were at least five thousand ball bearings in a pattern that would have taken out, or severely injured, every one within a thousand yards of the blast. It was the circuitry that was even more amazing though. There were no less than three mercury switches, any one of which could detonate the bomb if it were moved. There was also a circuit to command detonate the bomb if the timer failed, but that wasn't going to happen now. The bomb response unit had been jamming all frequencies since they were notified of the bomb.

Scanning from another location revealed several pressure censors. The censors were placed at key locations, so if the bomb was touched it would detonate. The arming and disarming was probably controlled remotely. There was no doubt the bomb was armed, but there was no way of knowing when it was set to go off. This wasn't the movies were the bomber has a convenient display showing the time left. All that showed here was a flashing LED confirming that the timer was running. They could only go by the tipster's detonation time of 10:15 p.m., and that was thirty minutes from now. The remote arming and disarming was ingenious. If someone associated with the band tried to move the bomb an observer could disarm it momentarily, and re-arm it after the threat of accidental detonation had passed.

"Five o five to headquarters."

"Headquarters. Go, five o five."

"We need all the Kevlar blast blankets you can find, and we need them five minutes ago!"

"Will do, five o five. Headquarters out."

The two men in the bomb squad van were monitoring the traffic between 505 and headquarters. They came crashing up to the stage in the van sending chairs flying in all directions. They bailed out of the van and started unloading blast blankets, handing them to the men on the stage. The men on stage made a tent frame out of guitar and drum stands. The blankets could then be put over the bomb without disturbing the pressure censors. Each van carried three blankets; 505 knew that wasn't nearly enough to contain the blast and the shrapnel inside the bomb. Three blankets would be blown aside like leaves in a sudden gust of wind on a fall day. Suddenly another two vans crashed through the chairs, one coming from the right, and the other from the left. That made a total of nine thirty-pound Kevlar blast blankets over the bomb. Whether nine blankets was enough or not was irrelevant now. According to the tipster: time was up.

EST 505 looked at his watch: 10:10 p.m. on the nose.

"Everybody take cover! Take cover!"

The police officers guarding the hotel lobbies and any hotel employees took cover in the offices behind the main desks. Just as everybody turned to leave, the supporting structure, because of the weight of the blankets, started to shift. Five o five was in a position to stop them, and he did. He realized that if he let go the structure would collapse, and the bomb would detonate killing him and all the men trying to escape. Five o five stayed there quietly holding the pile of blankets steady, so the men running to the vans could make their getaway. They all piled into a van of their choice. Then, each van took off in a different direction destroying what was left of the chairs. The vans all regrouped in a safe area behind a hotel. Suddenly someone noticed that 505 wasn't there.

"Five o five, what's your location? There's only two minutes to detonation."

Five o five answered, hurriedly explained the problem, and told everyone to stay put. Just as he finished talking there was a huge muffled explosion. Back on stage two minutes ago 505 was on the radio; two minutes later the bomb went off, and 505 along with everything else on stage took flight. Some of the debris crashed through hotel lobby windows, and some went as high as two- or three-story windows. Some ball bearings, escaping the blankets, riddled every building at ground level that was facing the stage. The damage, however, was minuscule compared to what would have happened if it weren't for 505 and his team.

The bomb squad members, ignoring procedure for re-entering a scene, sped back in their vans to search for 505. He wasn't answering the attempts to contact him on the radio. The vans came to a halt inside the square, and the men immediately bailed out and started to search for him. They hoped the combination of the blankets and his armored suit had saved his life.

Soon one of the guys shouted, "Over here! He's over here!" Everybody ran over to a building that was about five hundred feet from ground zero.

"Is he alive?" someone asked.

"Yes. That awning broke his fall. I think his leg and arm are broken, but that's all."

"Paramedics are on the way!" another team member said.

Soon 505 was headed for the hospital, and the federal crime scene investigation teams took over the scene.

Chapter Nine

Special Agent Dan Crenshaw opened his eyes and looked at the clock on his nightstand. It was 8 a.m., New Year's Day. He rolled over on his left side and looked at the beautiful woman sleeping next to him. Kelly had been his date for the New Year's Eve party at his section chief's house. Remembering the great time he had at the party with her brought a smile to his face. Dan considered himself privileged when she accepted his 2 a.m. invitation to coffee at his place. This wasn't their first date, there had been others, but their relationship never developed past the intimate friends stage. Dan couldn't let himself fall in love with anyone. He was married to his job. He rolled over on his back and was about to drift off to sleep again when his cell phone rang.

"Hello, Crenshaw here," he answered.

"Dan, I need you to fly to Boston to investigate a bombing."

Dan, recognizing his section chief's voice, asked, "A bombing, sir?"

"Yes. The blast was contained by a bomb squad but…" Dan's section chief told him the whole story. "Dan, the director of the FBI wants you to do a firsthand report for him."

Dan said, "Yes, sir. I'll catch the first flight out and be there sometime later today."

"No, that would take too long. I'll have a chopper standing by at the airport ready to go as soon as you get there. You're a good man, Crenshaw. I wish I had more like you, Dan; you're one of a kind."

"Thank you, sir," Dan said.

Dan fought back the urge to add "I think" to his "Thank you, sir."

Kelly awoke just then, and asked, "What's going on, Dan?"

"I got an assignment. I'm sorry, I can't spend the day with you like we planned."

"But we were going to relax and watch the Tournament of Roses parade on TV, and the Rose Bowl game later on."

"I know and I am truly sorry, but this is really important."

"Can't they send someone else?"

"The director asked for me personally; I couldn't very well refuse him. Please feel free to stay as long as you want. There's plenty of food and drink in the fridge; just make yourself at home."

"No thanks, I don't think so. I have my own home to go to. I can be lonely there just as well as here. I'll be leaving as soon after you as possible," Kelly said dejectedly.

Dan took a shower, dressed, packed a bag, kissed Kelly goodbye, and promised to make it up to her. He hailed a cab outside his apartment building ,and in forty-five minutes he was airborne headed for Copley Square in Boston.

Dan's chopper landed on the rooftop landing pad of the Hilton hotel opposite Copley Square. Even though the hotel had sustained damage it was still open for business. Dan had no trouble getting a room. Most of the patrons had checked out, either because of the bombing, or just because they had to go home after New Year's. Dan walked out of the front lobby of the hotel and into the street. The CSI teams had cleared the outer most of the blast area last night, so the businesses could start repairing their storefronts. The street, however, was still closed to conventional traffic. The square itself was cordoned off with yellow crime scene tape, and a uniformed police officer was stationed every twenty feet or so. Dan showed one of these officers his ID, and he let Dan go beyond the tape.

Dan slowly and carefully made his way through the obstacle course of broken chairs, smashed band equipment, and large and small pieces of the stage. After about ten minutes he arrived at ground zero of the blast. Once there, he recognized the profile of ATF Agent Josh Pittman, "Hi, Josh." Agent Pittman turned and smiled at Dan.

"Glad you could make the party, Dan," Josh said as he held out his hand.

"You look tired, Josh," Dan said as he shook his friend's hand.

"I am; I've been here all night."

"Wow! How'd you get here so fast?"

"You're not going to believe this, but the family and I decided to spend our New Year's Eve in Boston! In fact we had tickets to this concert. Our room is right up there on the fourth floor. I shudder to think of what might have happened if no one had taken the tip seriously. My family and I owe our lives to Deputy Director Hamilton, the EWS, the tipster, and the Boston bomb squad."

"What's Hamilton got to do with this?" Dan asked.

"Didn't they tell you? The local NSA agent wasn't going to take the threat as seriously as he should have. He thought it was a prank. Hamilton gave him specific orders, and demanded that they be carried out."

"What kind of specific orders?"

"He told him to cordon off a five-block area, to activate the EWS, announce the concert was canceled because of a terrorist threat, and to start searching for the bomb with dog search teams."

"He said five blocks? Not four or three, but five?"

"Yes."

"He said to cancel the concert, not delay it?"

"Yes."

"He said to cancel because of a terrorist threat?"

"Yes,"

"He said to search specifically with dog search teams?"

"Yes. Why all the questions?" asked Josh.

"Oh, I just want to get it right for my report. Sounds like Hamilton hit it right on the money."

"You bet he did, and my family and I are alive because of it."

"Well, I'm not going to argue that point with you. I am certainly very happy that you and your family are all right. Can I ask you one more question, Josh?"

"Sure."

"You're the expert here; if this bomb hadn't been contained how far would the blast effects been felt?"

"Well, we figured the bomb squads estimate of one hundred pounds of explosive was a little light. It was more like 125 pounds. So the blast would have been damaging up to a radius of four blocks, or a little more."

"What was the overall weight?" Dan queried.

"Including ball bearings, circuitry, and explosive, about 255 pounds."

"Wow! Not something you would carry nonchalantly up to the stage and drop off there."

"Nope," Josh agreed.

"How about the street exterior security cams, anything there?"

"We have people looking at the tapes, but we're not hopeful. The cams cover the sidewalks and streets, not the area behind the stage."

"So, you think it was terrorists, Josh?"

"Had to be. It fits the profile. Lots of soft targets, massive amount of explosive, and tamper proof housing."

"What about the tipster?"

"What about him?"

"Well, Al Qaeda members are fiercely loyal. They're not about to tip off the NSA or any other law enforcement agency."

"It could have been someone that overheard the plans and decided to call it in," Josh speculated.

"Maybe, but he would have had to have heard every detail down to the time the bomb was set to go off."

"Well Dan, that's not entirely unheard of you know. Same old Dan, always questioning the obvious."

"What can I say, it's my nature, that's all. Send me a copy of your report so I can include it with mine will you?"

"Sure thing, Dan. Anything else?"

"Now that you asked, is the NSA agent who took the call around?"

"Yeah, that's him right over there."

Josh pointed at a tall black man in a dark blue suit and tie with a parka over top.

"His name is Jim, or Jack, or something like that."

Dan walked over to were Jim or Jack was standing, and introduced himself.

"Glad to meat you, Agent Crenshaw, I've heard a lot about you. I'm Agent Jordan Smythe of the NSA. How can I help you?"

"I understand you took the original phone call from the tipster?"

"Yes I did," Jordan answered rather reservedly.

Dan noticed the inflection in his voice and said, "Don't worry, I'm not investigating your actions. Truth be told, I probably would have been skeptical of the call myself. What can you tell me about the caller? Did he have an accent, were there background noises, anything at all that comes to mind?"

"You know, you're the first person to ask me that question?"

This wasn't surprising to Dan; everybody here was convinced this was the work of terrorists.

"The guy definitely had an accent, but it sounded like a fake Middle East accent to me," Agent Smythe stated.

"Why do you think so?"

"I served three years in the gulf, and I married an Iraqi woman who has become a naturalized US citizen. Believe me, I know a true Middle East accent when I hear one!"

"Any background noises?"

"Sounded like a TV or radio playing in the background, but I couldn't make out what programs or even the language being spoken."

Dan thought to himself, *The radio in the background is an old CIA trick to confuse the listener from identifying background noises. There's that old specter of doubt again rearing its ugly head. Why do CIA techniques keep coming up in these investigations?*

107

"What about Deputy Director Hamilton?" Dan asked.

"What about him?"

"How did he sound to you? Was he nervous, surprised, sarcastic, what?"

"None of the above really. I am a graduate of the NSA Interrogation School, that's my main job, interrogation. It's been my job for the past three years. I was doing the agent on call a favor by taking his place while he spent the New Year's with his ailing father."

"OK, what did you notice about Hamilton?"

"You might think I'm crazy, but it seemed to me, by the tone in his voice, that he was expecting my call."

"Oh really?"

"Yes."

"Notice anything else?"

"Yes, when he gave me my orders, I think he had memorized them in advance. There is a certain rhythm to a person's voice when they have memorized what to say. That rhythm is very hard to mask completely."

"So you think you heard that in Hamilton's voice?"

"Well, I wasn't listening for it specifically, but it sure seemed like it. What does all this mean?" asked Agent Smythe.

"Oh, probably nothing, just my old curiosity kicking in. Don't worry about your response to the tip, I'm not mentioning it in my report."

"Thank you, sir," said Agent Smythe gratefully.

The rest of the day was spent interviewing CSI investigators and looking at literally a ton of debris. After he was finished, Dan went up to his room to sort out the notes he had taken and start his report. He opened his laptop on the table, but he could only sit and stare at it. He was distracted. It wasn't the evidence of the bombing that was bothering him. It was something else, something that he had been working on independently. He brought up the file marked HAM. Ham of course was short for Hamilton. Dan had started this file as soon as he heard Hamilton was appointed deputy director of the DHS. He remembered him from the gulf when Brad and he had a run-in with Hennery in the officers club. Dan didn't like him then, and he really didn't like him now! Dan paused for a second and wondered how Brad was getting along.

I really should take the time to get in touch with my old friend someday, he thought.

Dan looked at what he had compiled. His file started with a brief history of Hamilton's career. He had been second in command his whole career, and still is.

That could be a motive, he thought. *Maybe he wants the director's job, and is trying to make himself look good, and the director look bad. The EWS worked great, and everyone knows that was his idea.*

Dan entered the new evidence he had acquired today. Everything pointed to Hamilton knowing about the bombing in advance. He ordered dog search teams, because he knew that the bomb was too dangerous to move. If someone had tried to move it while searching it would have gone off prematurely. He cancelled the concert, because he knew the bomb couldn't be disarmed, and would have to be contained and detonated. He also mentioned terrorists so everyone would have a preconceived notion that terrorists were to blame. Dan had a weak circumstantial case at best; definitely not enough to bring any charges.

Dan continued his reasoning, *It was a sure bet that Hamilton didn't build the bomb, nor did he plant it in the square. It sure wasn't him on the videos from the Supreme Court Building either. He has people helping him; they're probably old CIA buddies. That's why CIA tactics keep popping up everywhere. I have to keep carefully digging on my own without raising suspicion. If these guys are ex-CIA they could take me out before I even knew they were on to me.*

Dan's train of thought was interrupted by a knock on his door. "Just a minute!" Dan hurriedly closed the file on his laptop and went to the door.

"Who is it?" Dan asked through the door.

"It's Josh," came the reply. Dan opened the door and let Josh in.

"I thought you'd be sound asleep by now," Dan said.

"Nah, you'd be surprised what a couple a gallons of coffee can do for you. Here's that copy of my report you wanted.."

"Thanks, I wasn't expecting it until tomorrow."

"Well, my family is still here, and I would like to show them some of the sights before we head for home in a couple of days."

"Trying to salvage the holiday, huh?"

"Yeah, what's left of it." Josh turned to leave but hesitated.

"Something more, Josh?" Dan asked.

"Dan, you've been asking a lot of questions about Hamilton. You know that might not be so good for your career: if you get my meaning?"

"No, I don't think I do, Josh."

"Hamilton and the DHS have a lot of influence and they can make or break a person."

"Don't you mean a person's career?"

"Yes, of course."

"Josh, since when is it wrong to ask questions in this country? The last time I looked we still had the first amendment in place."

"Look, Dan, I like you. I wouldn't want to see anything happen to you, or your career. You know, when a person loses their job sometimes they never recover. I just wouldn't want to see that happen to you; that's all."

"Well, I thank you for your concern, Josh, and I will certainly think about what you've said."

The two men shook hands. Dan thanked Josh again then closed and locked the door after him. If Dan had any doubts about Josh being in someone's pocket they were laid to rest. What he couldn't understand is how Hamilton could influence so many people for his own gain. Dan's instincts told him that there had to be more than just a promotion at stake here, but what could it be? Who were the people working for him and why? Were higher-ups involved, or were they his targets?

"Hell, with his ego, he might even think the presidency was within his reach!"

Dan needed some more information, and he had a pretty good idea who could supply some of it. Little did he know that a large piece of information would come from a completely unexpected source in the not so distant future.

The morning of January 3, 2022, found Dan in his office going over his mail and inter-office memos. He had some time to think about the case he had compiled against Hamilton. Dan had come to the conclusion that he needed a ton more evidence to bring any kind of charges against him. He couldn't accuse the deputy director of the DHS of a crime on circumstantial evidence, and he couldn't let him know in advance by making wild accusations. Hamilton could very easily cover his tracks and destroy vital evidence. It would be simple for an ex-CIA section chief to dispose of incriminating evidence. There was one other all too real reason for not ruffling his feathers prematurely. Dan considered himself too young to die.

"Deputy Director Hamilton's office. How may I help you?"

"Stephanie?" asked Dan.

"Speaking. Who is this?"

"You mean you don't recognize my voice? It's Dan."

"I recognized your voice; I was hoping I was wrong."

"Oh come on! You're not still mad about that weekend getaway last July are you?"

"What getaway? We spent one night in a beautiful seaside hotel. The next morning you were on your way to Alabama on an emergency assignment, and I was alone with twenty-five couples! I never saw you again until three weeks later."

" It was Arkansas, and the director called me in personally."

"Let's see, were have I heard that before. Oh yes! Yesterday when I called Kelly in records to see how her New Year's Eve date went with you. You know, it's too bad the FBI is so short of funds that they can only afford one agent!"

"Hey, can I help it if I'm the best of the best?"

"Oh, you don't want me to go there. So what, may I ask, is the purpose of your call, sir?"

"I have reservations for two at the Galileo, and I would like you to join me."

"Wow, that's a five-star restaurant. What are you going to do, propose?"

"No, I tried marriage once. It didn't work out."

"Gee, I wonder why? Hey, the boss just walked in. What time are you picking me up?"

"How about 7:30?"

"OK."

Stephanie and Dan walked through the front doors of the Galileo at 7:55 p.m. They were greeted by the hostess, and after checking their reservations, she escorted them to their table.

"How in the world did you get reservations for this place? I've heard of people waiting as long as a month for a reservation here."

"Well, sometimes it pays to be a special agent for the FBI, and get your name in the papers."

"It's too bad those times are so few and far between," countered Stephanie.

Their waiter came to their table, introduced himself, and gave them each a menu. He made his recommendations, and left them to make their choices.

After a delicious dinner, Dan and Stephanie sat at their table enjoying an after-dinner coffee. "OK, Dan, I know this evening isn't just about making up for last July. So what kind of favor do you need? Not that I don't appreciate this evening. Everything was perfect, right down to the company."

"Well thank you, and may I say you've made the evening perfect for me. But you're right, I do have an ulterior motive for this evening."

Dan informed Stephanie of the circumstantial case he had against Hamilton in detail.

"Why that egotistical son of a bitch. What do you think his master plan is?"

"That's one of the things you could help me with. If you want to, that is?"

"Oh, I have no love lost for Mr. Hamilton. I can see right through that Mr. Good Guy act of his. What do you want me to do?"

"Does he have any files that are for his eyes only that you could get a copy of?"

"He has a drawer that he keeps locked in the bottom of his desk. I've seen him take a folder out and look at it from time to time," answered Stephanie.

"That makes sense. He wouldn't keep sensitive information on his computer; it could be discovered if he were investigated. Computer files can never be totally destroyed, but paper can."

"So you want me to get a copy of what's in that folder?" asked Stephanie.

"You said he keeps the drawer locked."

"Did I ever tell you my father was a locksmith?"

"No, you left that little detail out of our conversations," Dan answered.

"He taught me how to pick a lock before I was out of grade school. I can get that folder no sweat."

"Hey, I don't want you to think this is some kind of game. These guys are serious bad news. If you get caught they will kill you. Make no mistake about it."

"I already took that into consideration, and I still want to help," Stephanie said reassuringly.

"OK, just be careful; be very careful."

The taxi dropped Dan and Stephanie off at her apartment building, and Dan walked Stephanie to her fourth-floor apartment.

Stephanie turned around to face Dan and said, "I had a wonderful evening, Dan. You know, a girl could fall head over heels for you very easily. But unfortunately you have another love, an all-consuming love, that I don't think you will ever get tired of, and that's a shame. If you ever do get tired of it, and decide to settle down, you know where I live."

Stephanie stretched upwards a little and gave Dan a kiss on the lips and a hug. Then she turned around, opened her apartment door, and disappeared inside closing the door behind her.

Chapter Ten

The music from the clock radio alarm crept into Brad's ear, awakening his brain. He was in that deep sleep one only falls into just before it's time to get up and go to work. He looked at the clock; it was 6 a.m., and this was Monday, January 4, 2022. Brad had enjoyed the fact that New Year's Day was on a Friday, giving him Saturday and Sunday off. Now the holidays were over and it was business as usual. He never liked getting up early for work, not even when he was in the Army. It was a different story altogether when he had to get up early for something fun.

"Come on, Brad, drag your sorry ass out of bed," he said to himself.

He wasn't looking forward to the weeks of overtime ahead. The money was good, but the money wasn't worth the time away from home and Mary. Brad took a shower, shaved, and got dressed for work. The alarm clock said 6:45 a.m.. It was time to head downstairs and see what Mary has for breakfast. Just as Brad walked into the kitchen the microwave's timer went off. He just shook his head, said good morning to Mary, and sat down at the kitchen table. After breakfast, he kissed Mary goodbye and left for work.

After Brad left, Mary went back upstairs and showered. She fixed her hair and did all the necessary things that women do to make themselves presentable to the world. On the way to work, after stopping for the morning paper, she recapped the holidays in her mind. Christmas was perfect; she couldn't describe it in any other way. Dad loved his gift of a puppy, and when she called him on New Year's Day both he and the puppy were doing fine. New Year's Eve was great. They had a wonderful time at Keesha and Bill's party. They met new people and got reacquainted with some former acquaintances. She and Brad volunteered to have the party at their house next year. All in all the holidays had been the best they'd experienced in a very long time.

Mary pulled into the school parking lot and parked in her space. After the usual stops she went to her classroom, and as usual she had a half hour before her first class filed in. She looked at the front page of the newspaper for the first time. On the front page was the headline "Bombing Investigation Completed." She read the article stating what she considered was the obvious. Terrorists had planted the bomb, and at press time the authorities had no suspects. The EWS had worked perfectly, and did exactly what it was supposed to do; warn people of impending danger. It even saved the life of an ATF agent and his family who had been spending the holiday weekend in Boston. It was now estimated that over one thousand people's lives were saved by the system. The one injury was a bomb squad commander. The paper said he's recovering in the hospital, and should be released in a couple of weeks. Just then the bell rang signifying the start of class, and her first class started filing in.

Brad pulled into the parking lot and parked under the cable company sign just like he always did. He clocked in and went to get his work orders for the day. Just then he heard a commotion out in the bay area and decided to investigate. A bunch of the guys were standing around excitedly talking about something. Brad walked up to Jim Rathburn and said, "What's up."

"Great news, Brad my boy! It seems that bombing scared the hell out of everybody in the country. They're coming in by the thousands to get the new cable boxes so they can install them themselves. It seems they don't want to wait for us to install them. They figure the boxes are too important for their family's safety to wait. That means the boxes will be in place at least a month, if not two months, early! No more overtime, Brad my man! We get to go home at a decent hour from now on in!"

Brad couldn't have been more elated. He really missed coming home to Mary at a decent hour and spending the evening with his favorite person in the whole wide world. Suddenly, Brad remembered Bill's father's words, "People will do anything to feel safe again."

The next few days were quite easy. There were lines of hundreds of people waiting to sign for their cable boxes. There wasn't much for installers to do until the computers could figure out who had boxes and who didn't. The cable services placed adds on TV asking anyone who wasn't going to install their own boxes to call in, and a technician would stop by with one. The number of installations for Brad and the other technicians dropped from twelve to eighteen a day down to two or three. Brad was getting home at the decent hour of 5 or 6 p.m., and no out-of-town overnight stays. It was like a miracle. If he could find the terrorists who planted that bomb he'd give them each a medal! He even got around to installing their personal cable boxes, one for the living room TV, and one for the bedroom TV.

Paul Lorinsky felt something warm, wet, and rough rubbing his cheek. He opened his eyes and saw a huge black nose and two beady eyes looking him dead in the face. It was 7 a.m. and Big Dog needed to go out. Paul got out of bed, put on his jeans, sweatshirt, boots, coat, hat, grabbed Big Dog's leash, and they both headed outside. He took the dog to the back yard and gave him the command to do his thing. After a short bit of exploration Big Dog complied, and both owner and dog headed back into the house. Paul looked at the calendar on the kitchen wall. It was Tuesday, January 5, 2022, the day he told himself he would go to town and pick up one of those infernal cable boxes and install it. The cable company strung the cable wires past his house last week. Then they ran a cable to a junction box they installed on his house. Now he had to run a cable from that junction box to the inside of his house and hook it up to the cable box he was bringing home today.

After getting cleaned up, he and Big Dog ate breakfast. Then they both piled into his pickup truck and headed for town. Paul pulled into the cable company's parking lot and noticed that there were only three customers waiting in line. That was one of the advantages of living near a small town; no crowds. He had heard that in the larger cities the lines were hundreds of people deep. He left Big Dog in the truck happily chewing on his rubber chew toy, and got in line. The dog would be fine in the truck. The temperature was thirty degrees and the sky was overcast. About thirty minutes later Paul came back to the truck with his new cable box.

"Man," he said to himself. "It was like buying a house, all the forms and signing I had to do. Then there were the warnings of penalties under the law. What the hell is this thing made out of, platinum?"

About 1 p.m., Paul pulled his pickup truck into his driveway and turned off the ignition. He took Big Dog to the back yard were he promptly peed, and then put him in the house. He went back to the pickup and carried the cable box into the house. He looked the thing over. It looked like any other cable box on the outside. The inside is were all the goodies are. He fought the urge to take the cover off, and set it down beside the TV. After an hour of work, stringing the cable from outside to the new box, he screwed the cable onto the box. Then he plugged the box into the wall outlet, and then plugged the TV into the cable box, just like they told him to do at the cable office. Then he took the HDMI cable and ran it from TV to the cable box. He turned on the TV, and as soon as the box ran its setup program he was in business.

"Well, Big Dog, I guess we'll be watching our favorite shows tonight." Big Dog looked at Paul, tilted his head to show that he recognized his own name, and then returned to chewing on his toy.

The next morning after the chores had been taken care of, Paul was in his electronics workshop. He had purchased a mini-cam a few months ago on the end of a long, flexible cable. He thought it might come in handy looking into cramped and tight places, such as drains to see what's clogging them, and inside electronic devices without taking them apart. They said he couldn't "move, tamper with, or take the cover off the cable box." They didn't say he couldn't look inside it! He brought the apparatus into his living room and set the small monitor where he could see it easily. Then he turned the camera on and pushed the camera cable into a ventilation hole in the cable box casing. He explored inside the box being very careful not to bump any electronic circuits with the metal cable. What he saw was nothing short of amazing. It was the most advanced example of micro and conventional circuitry he had ever seen. It was state of the art. Actually it was a little beyond state of the art, absolutely magnificent.

He probed and watched the monitor like a man at his first pornographic peep show. He was totally fascinated. He sent the probe to the front of the box and could see the connectors that went to the various switches and controls. He was about to pull out, when something in the right front corner caught his attention. He went in for a closer look and couldn't believe his eyes. It was a black box. The black box was about one and a quarter inches square. It was plugged into a socket like they used to use for central processors in computers.

"What in the world is that dinosaur doing in this better-than-state-of-the-art circuit? A black box; what was it's purpose?" Paul said out loud.

He often talked to himself when he was alone. Some people say it's a sign of genius, others say it's a sign of insanity; actually there is only a fine line separating the two. Paul studied the black box for a while. It had no apparent seams, and it seemed to be made of some nonconductive material.

Paul got an idea. He remembered the camera had a miniature microphone attached. He turned the mike on, and very carefully put it against the black box. The speaker on the monitor started humming. Well, whatever this thing was it was functioning, and it sounded like it was putting out some kind of signal.

"But what kind of signal? Was it receiving, or transmitting, or both?" he said as he thought out loud. Well, that's all he could learn without taking the cable box apart, and that was out of the question "under penalty of law," he said sarcastically. "It's time to take Big Dog for his afternoon walk anyway."

The next day turned out to be an unseasonably warm day for January. Paul had to make a run to the feed store and get a bag of dog food for Big Dog. He parked in the feed store parking lot and got out of his pickup. He hadn't taken the dog with him because the temperature had gone up to fifty degrees, and the sun was shining. It would get too hot for the dog in just a few seconds in the cab of the pickup, so he left him at home. He walked through the door of the old feed store. The old wooden floor planks made a hollow sound as he walked across them. There was an old potbellied stove by the checkout counter with a dying fire going in it. The whole scene reminded him of less complicated times, when life was slower and more relaxed.

Paul looked around at all the different types of feed they sold. Everything from rabbit feed to horse feed. He walked over to the all-natural dog food, picked up a forty-pound bag, and carried it over to the checkout counter.

"Where's Fred?" Paul asked the man behind the counter.

"Fred got the flu. I'm his nephew George from Youngstown. I was visiting for the holidays, and decided to extend my stay to help him out."

"Well, that's real nice of you, George. Glad to meet you. I'm Paul. Fred told me he had a sister and nephew in Youngstown that were coming to visit for the holidays."

"It's nice to meet you, Paul; Uncle Fred told me a lot about you."

"Good things, I hope?"

"Oh yes, sir, nothing but the best. That comes to nineteen dollars and eighty-four cents with tax."

Paul handed the young man a twenty and got his dollar and six cents back in change. "Well, if I don't see you again it was nice meeting you, and tell Fred to get well real soon."

"I sure will, and thanks for your purchase."

Paul waved as he carried the bag of dog food out the door. He threw the dog food bag into the truck bed, went around to the driver's side, and got in behind the wheel. Paul pulled his pick up onto the paved country road and headed for home. He didn't notice the silver SUV pulling out right behind him. Paul was too preoccupied to notice the vehicle, because something about the price of the dog food rang a bell.

He started reasoning out loud, "Nineteen eighty-four, let's see, that was a good year as well as I can remember. Hmmm, 1984, 1984, nothing spectacular happened that year that I can remember."

It's amazing how the mind never shuts down. It's always processing, always reasoning, even when you're not conscious of it. That's what happened to Paul that day.

"Wait a minute! *1984*, Big Brother, my God can it be true? Yes! Why not! They have the technology!"

Dad took out his cell phone. He had to call someone about this! He had Brad's cell phone number on speed dial. "Yes, I'll call him and tell him, he'll know what to do!"

In the SUV following Paul, two men wearing wireless headsets were listening to the bug they planted in the pickup, and looked at each other with concern.

"Fire that thing up! He's figured it out!" yelled the driver.

The man in the passenger seat flipped the switch on what could only be described as a ray gun rifle. It had a long plastic tube for a barrel with thousands of copper coils inside. It had a trigger, and a stock for aiming; it looked for all the world like a ray gun from an ancient Buck Rogers movie. The weapon made a high-pitched whine as the batteries charged the capacitors. The guy riding shotgun stuck the weapon out the window and took aim.

Back in the pickup Paul heard Brad's cell ringing, but Brad didn't answer; his service picked up. After the message and the beep Paul started to talk excitedly, "Brad this is Dad, listen, I figured out what they're doing, it's *1984*, Big Brother, a black box in…"

Suddenly the engine of the truck died. Paul tried to restart it while it was still rolling, but it wouldn't even try to turn over. He looked at his cell phone and it was dead too, and so were all of the instruments and gauges on his dash. He guided the truck to the edge of the road, and turned on his hazard warning lights, but they didn't work either. Even his battery-operated digital watch had gone blank. He was puzzled to say the least. What had happened? Paul suddenly realized that he wasn't alone. He looked in his rearview mirror, and saw that a silver SUV had pulled up behind his pickup.

A man got out of the SUV and walked up to the truck's driver's side, and showed his ID to Paul. He was a sheriff's deputy; the picture ID and badge looked genuine. Paul couldn't roll down the power windows, so he opened the door and got out.

"Having trouble with your truck?" the deputy asked.

"Yes, I can't understand it, nothing works."

"Probably a loose battery cable. Let's check under the hood."

Both men went to the front of the truck and popped the hood. Paul grabbed one of the cables. Suddenly an enormous electric shock rendered him unconscious in just a few seconds. The phony sheriff's deputy pulled the darts, with wires connected to them, out of Paul's jacket where they had stuck. He put away the taser that he had disabled his victim with and waved to his accomplice.

"Watch out for traffic while I finish him off," he said.

The man sat Paul's body up and leaned it against the bumper. He took Paul's right hand and placed it on his chest. He then loosened the battery cable from the battery and took a syringe out of a small case. He injected a clear fluid into the membrane on the inside of Paul's nose.

"What's that?" asked the accomplice.

"Digitalis, it's used for slowing down a rapid irregular heart beat. In the case of a healthy heart a normal dose can stop the heart altogether: bingo, instant heart attack. Can't be traced even if they knew to look for it."

"Why up the nose?"

" Lots of blood vessels to pick it up and carry it to the heart, but a virtually undetectable injection sight."

"Geez, you're diabolical! No wonder they call you Dr. Death."

"OK, no pulse, no respiration; let's get the hell out of here!" Both men ran back to the SUV, jumped in, and sped off.

Brad pulled into the driveway of their humble abode at about 5:30 p.m. after a rather mild day at work. He stopped his pickup about five feet behind Mary's SUV and climbed out. The weather was mild for January 5, he thought; only fifty degrees. He opened the kitchen door and noticed immediately that something was wrong. There wasn't anything cooking on the stove, and it sounded like voices in the living room.

He said "hello" from the kitchen so as not to startle anyone. When he entered the living room he grew even more concerned.

Mary was sitting on the sofa with Keesha. Keesha had her arm around Mary, and Mary was crying. Brad ran over to her, sat down beside her, and asked her what had happened?

Mary looked up at him, and managed to get out the words "He's gone" between sobs.

"Who's gone?" Brad asked quietly.

Keesha looked at him with tear-reddened eyes and said, "Your father-in-law has passed."

Keesha might as well have hit Brad in the chest with a sledgehammer. It took all his strength just to breathe, and console Mary by putting his arm around her. He had lost two sets of parents in his lifetime now, and it was almost too much for him to bear. The only thing that held him together was the fact that Mary needed him. She was hurting more than he was, and she needed his help.

There was a knock at the door, and Keesha went to answer it. It was Bill; he said, "I got your message. How is everyone?"

"Not good, as you can imagine."

Bill put his arm around his wife, and they went into the living room to be with Mary and Brad. They sat quietly in the living room for about an hour, then Mary looked up and said, "Thank you both for coming over."

"No need for thanks," Bill said. "When did this happen?" he asked.

Mary answered, "They're not sure. The sheriff's office called about 4:30 p.m. with the news. He was found with his truck on the side of the road. They think it was a heart attack."

"Why didn't you call me, sweetie?" Brad asked.

"We tried, but you didn't answer."

"Oh damn, we had a meeting at two o'clock. I put my phone on silent, and forgot to take it off. I am so sorry."

"That's OK, Brad, you couldn't have know," Mary said comfortingly.

"Keesha, you and Bill can go home. Brad's here now. I'll be OK."

"OK, but if you need anything don't you hesitate to call."

Keesha and Bill gave Mary a hug in turn. Then Keesha gave Brad a hug also. Bill shook Brad's hand, then hugged him and gave him a pat on the back. After closing the front door Brad turned to Mary and hugged her. He had managed to hold back the tears until now, but now the tears flowed freely over his cheeks. A great man had passed away. Brad admired Dad as much as any childhood hero he'd ever heard of. Tomorrow, he'd call in and take a week off because of a death in the family. They'd pack their clothes and make the hardest trip of their lives. Brad knew Dad wasn't going to live forever, but he thought he would be around for at least another ten years. It just didn't make sense; Dad was in perfect health! Even while Brad was grieving, he was suspicious of the explanation given for Dad's death.

Brad drove Mary's SUV to Dad's house the next day while Mary slept for a few hours on the way. She hadn't slept the night before, and Brad was glad to see her finally get some rest. He pulled into Dad's driveway and parked behind Donald's van. Mary woke up, and they both went inside to see Donald and his family. Some of the neighbors were there to help in any way they could. Dad had prepared for his passing by making all the arrangements ahead of time. The relatives all spent the night at Dad's house. Somehow it seemed less painful with all of them together. It was like Dad hadn't passed away at all, but was there comforting each one of them.

The next day after breakfast they sat around talking about old times and meeting neighbors who brought food and condolences. Soon, it was time to go to the funeral home for calling hours. There was an honor guard from the local American Legion post, and many of Dad's neighbors came in from all over to pay their respects. At the end of the evening the whole family stood by the open coffin, and gave Dad their farewell one at a time.

Reverend Woodward conducted the funeral service the next day. After the service the pallbearers carried the coffin to the hearse. The procession of vehicles slowly made its way out of the funeral home parking lot and to the cemetery. Soon, Dad would be laid to rest next to his beloved Cynthia. They would be together again now for all eternity. At the grave site Reverend Woodward spoke of Dad's faith in the Lord, and how we who believe will be together again in heaven. The American Legion honor guard fired a twenty-one-gun salute. The flag that was draped over the coffin was folded and given to Donald being the oldest next of kin. After the graveside service, Reverend Woodward asked Mary if he could speak to Brad for a moment, and she consented.

"Brad," Reverend Woodward began, "your father-in-law started a work that he never finished. I know it was the Lord's work. It's up to you to finish that work. I'm sorry to say Donald is not of the same spirit as his father. So the responsibility falls on you. Be open to the spirit of God, and he will guide you." Brad felt like every word Reverend Woodward said was branded into his brain and would never be forgotten.

The day after the funeral was Friday. Because everyone had just a week before they went back to work, the decision was made to have the reading of the will that afternoon. Dad's attorney drove out to the house for the reading. There were no surprises in the will. Dad's assets were divided evenly between Donald and Mary. Dad left five thousand dollars each towards the two grandsons' college fund.

Saturday was spent going through Dad's personal items, and the usual things families do when a member passes away. In fact it took until Monday morning to figure out who got what, and what would be given to charity. Both Donald and Mary decided that Brad should get Dad's electronic equipment.

At one time during the decision making Brad decided to head for the kitchen to get a cold Coke out of the fridge. Anna was in the kitchen with the boys. The two boys decided to go outside and explore leaving Brad and Anna alone to talk.

"How are you holding up? I know Paul was like a father to you," asked Anna.

"Oh, I'm a lot better than I was a couple of day's ago, that's for sure. How's Donald taking it?"

"He's doing pretty good. I know he's hiding a lot of the pain though. You know he and his father didn't see eye to eye on a lot of things, but he's still hurting. He just got promoted to sergeant after only eight years on the force. He planned to tell Paul this weekend, and I know he's heartbroken about not getting the chance."

"Well, if it's any consolation to him, I firmly believe that Dad knows, and approves of his accomplishment."

With a tear in her eye, she thanked Brad and said she would tell Donald what he said.

Tuesday morning Brad asked Mary if she minded if he went into town. He needed to talk to the sheriff about getting Dad's truck out of the impound. She said OK. Brad also asked Mary about Big Dog's whereabouts. Mary said that a neighbor volunteered to keep him until they decided if they wanted him or not. Brad asked Mary if it would be all right with her to take the dog home with them. She said that would be fine with her.

On the way into town Brad decided to check the messages on his cell phone. He hadn't checked messages since before the news about Dad's death. When he looked at the screen his blood ran cold. The first message was from Dad. The time stamp of the message was 2:35 p.m. January 5, about the time they said he was heading home from the feed store. Brad stopped the SUV at the side of the road and played the message.

"Brad, this is Dad. Listen, I figured out what their doing, it's *1984*, Big Brother, a black box in…"

The message ended abruptly. Brad wondered why. *What was Dad talking about? 1984, Big Brother, was Donald involved somehow? Nah, he couldn't be, it must mean something else. Where is this black box he's talking about? He said, "in"; in what? His house, his truck, his garage, where?* Brad saved the message. All the other messages were just what he thought they would be, condolences from co-workers and friends.

Brad pulled up in front of the sheriffs headquarters and parked in one of the diagonal parking spaces. A dispatcher at the front desk asked him if he needed help. Brad explained who he was, and was told to have a seat until the sheriff was available. After about ten minutes Sheriff Spangler came out of his office, shook Brad's hand, and invited him in.

"How can I help you, Mr. Spencer? Oh, first let me offer my condolences. I am very sorry for your loss. Now, how can I help you?"

"I'd like to know the details of my father-in-law's death."

"I wish I could tell you exactly what happened, but I can't. I can only speculate. It looked like your father-in law's truck broke down. He got out to see what went wrong, and while pulling on the battery cable it came loose throwing him of balance. Somehow he must have grounded himself completing a circuit, and sustained a high-level shock. The shock must have triggered a heart attack."

"Dad was the picture of health. I can't see him having a heart attack from an electric shock."

"Well, we had the state CSI guys check the scene for any evidence of foul play and they found none."

"Any tire tracks other than Dad's pickup?"

"The road this occurred on was paved; even the shoulders. There were no tire tracks from any vehicles."

"Was there an autopsy?"

"Yes. Since this is a closed case I can give you copies of my report and the coroner's report."

"Thank you, Sheriff, that would be very helpful, and how about the CSI report too?"

"Sure thing," said Sheriff Spangler.

The sheriff returned after a few minutes and handed Brad a folder of papers. Brad was about to leave when a question popped into his head.

"Sheriff? Did they ever find out what went wrong with Dad's truck?"

"I had the department's mechanic check it out. He said it was the damndest thing he'd ever seen. Every circuit and computer chip was fried. All he could say was that it must have been one hell of a short. Oh, that reminds me, I have your father-in-law's personal effects here. I guess it will be all right if you sign for them."

"Why did what happened to Dad's truck remind you of his effects?"

"Because his watch and cell phone are in the same condition."

Brad looked at both the cell phone and the watch. "Sheriff, do you know what an electromagnetic pulse, or EMP is?"

"I think so. It's an electrical phenomena usually associated with nuclear explosions. It can wipe out electronic equipment for quite a distance from ground zero."

"Right, but there has been some experimentation with EMPs as a weapon. By using a kind of EMP cannon."

"Yes, I've read about such weapons in the *Police Gazette*, but they're still in the experimental stages."

"Not anymore," Brad said to himself, "not anymore."

Brad thanked the sheriff for his help and asked for directions to the coroner's office. Brad knocked on the coroner's office door. "Come in," came the response from inside. Dr. Sheppard, the coroner, was a graying man of about fifty-five years old. He wore the traditional white smock over his white shirt, tie, and dark brown pants. He was seated at his desk, and when Brad walked in, he looked over the top of his reading glasses and said, "Can I help you, young man?"

Brad introduced himself and explained his purpose for being there.

"I wish I could tell you more than you already know, son, but I can't. I checked the body for any signs of foul play from head to toe. There were no marks, puncture wounds, bruises, or any defensive wounds on the body. The only peculiar thing I could find was the fact that your father-in law's heart and arteries were in very good shape for his age. The cause of death, as I listed on my report, was cardiac arrest. His heart just stopped beating for no apparent reason that I could find."

"Did he have any burn marks on his body?" Brad asked.

"Burn marks?"

"Yes, like from an electrical shock."

"Like I said, I checked the whole body from head to toe; there were no suspect marks whatsoever."

"Well that blows the sheriff's theory out of the water."

"The sheriff's theory?" asked Dr. Sheppard.

"Yes, he thinks Dad sustained a severe electric shock from his car battery that induced his heart attack."

"Unless your father-in-law was standing knee deep in water, there is no way he could have sustained a heart-stopping shock from a car battery!"

"I didn't think so either. Thank you for your time, Dr. Sheppard."

"No problem; my pleasure, son."

Brad went to the impound yard next and searched Dad's truck for the mysterious black box, to no avail. He made arrangements to have the truck towed to the dealership for repair. Dad had bought the extended warranty and the dealership said it would take at least six to eight weeks to complete the repairs. Brad gave them his cell phone number with instructions to call him when the repairs were complete. On the way home, Brad checked out the scene of the incident, and everything was like the sheriff said: No sign of a struggle or any other kind of foul play. The only thing Brad had that proved it was no accident, at least to him anyway, was the EMP weapon that was used. He was dead certain it was no accident.

The ride home gave Brad a chance to make a couple decisions. One: he wasn't going to tell Mary about what he had found out. He knew it would only upset her, and more upset is the last thing she needed right now. Two: he wasn't going to tell Donald either. Donald was thoroughly convinced that the federal government could do no wrong. It would be like talking to the wall. Brad also had a chance to speculate on how the murder was accomplished. Of course, more critical than how, was why?

What had Dad found out that warranted such drastic action? What on earth did Big Brother, 1984, and black box have to do with each other? Brad made a resolution to find out.

Chapter Eleven

"OK you guys, listen up," said Hennery. He was addressing the members of the dirty dozen meeting in a rented office space he kept just for that purpose. "Everybody here? Dick?"

"Yo."

" Bob?"

"Yo."

"Zeke?"

"Yah."

"Tom?"

"Here."

"Dave?"

"Yo."

"Bill?"

"Here."

"George?"

"Yah."

"Doc?"

"Here."

"Tad?"

"Present."

"Jake?"

"Uhu."

"Pete?"

"Yah."

"And Harry?"

"Here."

"First, I want to commend Bob and Dick on a great job at the Supreme Court Building. Next, a commendation and kudos go out to Doc and George for the perfect hit on Lorinsky. Last but certainly not least, Zeke, Tom, Jake, and Pete for the Copley Square bombing. Fantastic work! Very professional! I thank you from the bottom of my heart, and my pocket book." Hennery threw twelve envelopes down on the table in front of him. Each envelope contained 30,000 dollars in cash.

"That's just a bonus, guys, over and above your normal salary. Now, I have another job for three of you. Tad, Bill, and Harry, you guys are going to go on a raid of a terrorist cell. Well, at least it's going to look like a terrorist cell after you guys get through planting the evidence. You'll go in as DHS agents, and while the NSA agents are busy with the arrest, you guys will be planting evidence for CSI to find. The suspects are Islamic extremists who meet every Tuesday evening to watch TV, curse the United States and the president, whom they call the great pig. I don't think they should be doing that, do you? I didn't think so. You'll meet up with the other agents at 8 p.m. tomorrow at NSA headquarters. Your cover will be that you are from the DHS sent to observe the raid. Here's your ID's, they're genuine, the names aren't. You'll plant the same kind of explosives we used in both bombings, some ball bearings, and some micro-detonators. That ought to do the trick. I've already given the address to the NSA, and they'll have the details worked out by tomorrow night. I know you guys are pros, and you won't let me down."

"No, sir," the trio said simultaneously.

"Sir?"

"Yes, Doc."

"Sir, the old guy Lorinsky?"

"Yes, what about him?"

"He might have gotten a partial message off to his son-in-law over his cell phone before we took him out."

"What's this son-in-law's name?"

"Brad Spencer, Ohio plate TWD 4975, that might be his wife's tag number; her name is Mary."

"OK, I'll check him out. Any other business? OK, you guys stay low. I will have more work for you shortly."

Hennery was at his desk on Tuesday morning bright and early as usual. He fired up his computer and sat back sipping a cup of coffee while it booted up. After boot up, he went to the Bureau of Motor Vehicles screen and selected Ohio. He soon had Brad and Mary's address, phone numbers, both cell and land line, and most importantly Brad's SSN He ran Brad's SSN and found out exactly who he was, his qualifications, and service record. When his service photo came up, Hennery thought the guy looked familiar, but couldn't place him. Hennery placed Brad on his people to watch list, placed it in his bottom right-hand drawer and locked it. He picked up his cell phone, and punched in a speed-dial number. He didn't acknowledge anyone at the other end, he just spoke, "Bradley Spencer, number 216-555-7809 priority one," and hung up.

"All right, gentlemen, listen up. We have three new faces joining us tonight," the NSA assault team leader said as he pointed at Tad, Bill, and Harry. He read the phony names off the ID cards they gave him to introduce them to the rest of the team.

"They're here from the DHS to observe and assist us if needed. They are trained in assault tactics, so they won't get in the way. OK, the guys we are going after are suspected of the two most recent bombings in this country. They are Islamic extremists, and could be heavily armed. We have the element of surprise on our side, and I plan to keep it that way. We will make our approach from the north end of the street. Drivers, listen up, lights out and engines turned off two houses before the target house. We will coast as far as our momentum will carry us. When the vans stop, squad one will quickly proceed to the front door; squad two will proceed to the back door. When squad two reaches the back door and is in assault position, the squad leader will give the command 'take down.' At which point both door busters will fire simultaneously, or as close to it as possible. This should stun everyone inside for at least forty-five seconds. That's more than enough time for us to move in and secure the suspects. Any questions? OK, it's 19:30, time to load up!"

The ride to the target house took about fifty minutes. It took the two assault squads about two minutes to get into position, and then the squad two commander gave the command "take down."

The door busters were launched from their tubes, and when the projectiles hit their targets, the wooden entry doors literally disintegrated. The door busters were quite a weapon. Depending on the type of charge used, they could quite literally blow a solid steel door completely off its hinges. The shock wave usually keeps anyone from moving for at least forty-five seconds. A few suspects usually get injured, but not seriously, and of course the officers have the full protection of Patriot Act 2. After all, these are terrorist suspects, so the officers are immune from prosecution of any kind, even if they have the wrong house!

"Down! Everybody down!" both assault teams hollered as they charged into the house. All five occupants in the house were so stunned and afraid they went to the floor on top of each other for lack of space. The rest of the house was checked out and declared clear. While the two squads took care of the prisoners, the three phonies did their dirty work. Tad stood watch while Bill and Harry planted the evidence. They smeared traces of explosives on the surface of the kitchen table. Then they dropped crumbs of the stuff in the corners of the living room. They planted ball bearings in the kitchen drawer, and two micro-detonators in a pill bottle in a bathroom cabinet. It was true that these guys were Islamic extremists. They had a picture of Osama Bin Laden on the wall like he was some kind of deity. There were anti-American slogans written in Arabic on either side of the picture. Now, with the planted evidence, the suspects' fates were sealed.

"Well, how'd we do?" the assault leader asked of Tad.

Tad said, "Huh? Oh! Your guys did great; top notch; very professional. You can be proud of your team and yourself. We'll be giving a glowing report to our boss; you can count on it."

The prisoners were piled into a prisoner transport vehicle, and everyone else loaded up in the two original vans they had arrived in. The ride back was more relaxed and a lot less tense than the ride to the target house. There was lots of chatter, laughing, and camaraderie all around. Everybody patted each other on the back for a job well done.

Wednesday morning found Special Agent Dan Crenshaw stopping at his favorite café to read his newspaper and drink a coffee before heading for the office. The headlines caught his eye as it did everyone who bought the paper that morning. "Terrorist Cell Busted, Suspects Believed Guilty of Bombings!" While he sipped his coffee, he read the story of the assault on the terrorist house. Because of the Patriot Act not many details were given about the raid. The authorities did say that every detail of the military tribunal trial would be available to the press. They also said that if the suspects were convicted the punishment would be disclosed. Dan read the entire article and decided to look into the investigation firsthand as it develops. Dan walked to his car after finishing his coffee and drove the rest of the way to his office.

Entering his office, Dan sat behind his desk and tore yesterday's page off the daily calendar so it read, Wednesday, January 12, 2022. As a special agent for the FBI assigned to terrorism, Dan had certain privileges afforded to him that a regular agent wouldn't have. For example, being able to get any information about a raid on a terrorist house as soon as it was available. He made some phone calls to the NSA and the Federal Forensics Laboratory requesting that information and evidence reports be faxed to him as soon as possible. They said they would fax the reports over as soon as they were completed.

Dan's phone rang as soon as he hung it up. "Hello. Crenshaw here."

"Hi, Dan. It's Stephanie."

"Hi, babe. What's up?"

"I have that information you wanted."

"You mean on that ocean getaway bed-and-breakfast we were talking about?"

Stephanie, knowing full well inter-office as well as all phone calls were monitored and recorded, played along.

"Yes, when do you want to pick it up?"

"How about tonight around 7:30?"

"OK by me. See you then."

Dan hung up and started working on the mountain of paperwork in front of him. The next time he looked up it was 12:30 p.m., time for lunch. When he got back from lunch there was a faxed report from the NSA on his desk.

That was fast, he thought.

Dan read the report filed by the assault leader. The report was well written and detailed. They had surprised five suspects and taken four directly into lockup. The fifth had received minor injuries, and was treated in the emergency room and then taken to lockup. One peculiar thing caught Dan's attention. The list of officers that took part in the raid included three DHS agents. Dan was puzzled.

"Since when do DHS agents take part in assaults on terrorist strongholds?"

The report said that they were there to observe and assist if necessary. He supposed that could have been the case, but as far as he knew, DHS agents didn't get training in takedowns. Dan was suspicious. He looked at the names and ages of the suspects, and was greatly surprised. Two of the suspects were eighteen, two more were nineteen, and the last was twenty. Those ages seemed a little young to be making a sophisticated bomb like the one in Boston; never mind the bombing of the Supreme Court Building in Washington. Something was wrong, his instincts told him; very wrong.

Around 4:30 p.m., Dan got the forensics report on the raid. According to the report trace amounts of explosives were found in the living room and the kitchen of the terrorist house. When the explosives were analyzed, they were of the same type and chemical makeup as the explosives used in the two bombings. In fact the report said that there was a ninety-nine percent probability that the explosives found in trace amounts in the house were from the same batch. The report went on to say that ball bearings were found of the same size, weight, and grade as the ones from the Boston bomb. In the bathroom was found two micro-detonators in the bottom of an aspirin bottle. It's not what was in the report that caught Dan's attention, but what was missing. The report said that a few very small pieces of explosives were found in corners of the kitchen and living room. Nowhere in the report was there a mention of petroleum jelly.

If the bombs were made in that house as the evidence suggests, why weren't there trace amounts of petroleum jelly on any of the surfaces, the micro-detonators, or on the small amounts of explosives? Dan's investigative radar was on full alert now. *This was very suspicious; very suspicious indeed.*

Dan looked at the clock on the wall of his office; it read 6:45 p.m. He had just enough time to put the reports in his briefcase and head for the door. He pulled up and parked in front of Stephanie's apartment building at about 7:25 p.m. He took the elevator to her floor, and in a few seconds was knocking on her door.

"Who is it?" Stephanie asked.

"It's Dan." There was the sound of three locks unlocking and the door opened.

"I presume you used your peephole and made sure it was me before you opened the door?"

"Well of course I did! I might be crazy but I'm not stupid!"

"Good. Now where's the info you got for me? You're sure Hamilton doesn't suspect you of anything?"

"I can't see how he could. I opened the lock without leaving a single scratch, and locked it in the same manner. I was wearing gloves the whole time. I made copies of everything, and returned them to the file in exactly the same order as I found them."

"Good girl," said Dan.

"You know, you owe me big time for this, Dan?"

"I sure do, and I will pay you back; that's a promise. Let's see what you've got." Dan took all the papers out of the folder. There were twelve sheets of paper with a different picture of a man and his qualifications listed.

"Who are they?" asked Stephanie.

"They look like ex-CIA personnel to me judging from their qualifications. There are twelve of them; looks like a Dirty Dozen."

"Dirty Dozen?"

"It's from an old classic World War Two movie of the same name." Dan thought for a moment then asked Stephanie, "You know what this is? This is Hamilton's private army. You can believe me when I say twelve ex-CIA operatives are an army. These guys are capable of doing anything, and I think they've been busy little beavers in the past two months."

"You think they're responsible for the bombings don't you?"

"Yep, it sure looks like it. Is this all there was?"

"No, there's this handwritten list of names here."

Dan took the sheet of paper from Stephanie and studied it.

"These are the names of the five suspects that were apprehended last night. Look at the details of each of their lives. He knows things about them their best friend doesn't know."

"For example?" Stephanie asked.

"The eighteen-year-old likes black girls; he's dating one outside his neighborhood. Number ten: fornication. That's something his family or friends would never tolerate. This nineteen-year-old keeps pornography DVDs in his bedroom and watches them on his computer when his parents aren't home. Number eight: disrespect to parents. The twenty-year-old whose house was their meeting place is a closet gay; he has an eighteen-year-old boyfriend. Number eleven:

Homosexuality. The boyfriend is one of the arrested suspects. Looks like he couldn't get anything on the last one so he made something up. Number sixty-nine: Spying for enemies of Islam."

"What are these numbers?" asked Stephanie

"These things are from the seventy major sins of Islam. The numbers are where they rank in the list. What I want to know is how did Hamilton pick these guys, and get such sensitive info on them? This is stuff they would never talk about to anyone in their family or cultural group, that's for sure."

Dan went down the list. Suddenly his eyes widened and his face lost some color.

"Bradley Spencer, wife Mary, father-in law Paul Lorinsky, and their complete addresses. What are they doing on this list?!"

"Who's Bradley Spencer?" asked Stephanie.

"If it's the same Brad Spencer, he's an old army buddy that I haven't seen in years. Funny thing, I was wondering about him just the other day. I'll have to look him up at the office when I get to work tomorrow. One thing is certain, his name on this list can't be good. If I could find out how Hamilton gets his information it would go a long ways toward upsetting his apple cart. The house that was raided looked like any other house from the outside. Out of all the thousands of houses in the area how did Hamilton know that Islamic extremists met there on Tuesday at 8:00 p.m.?"

"Maybe the guy that he listed with sin number sixty-nine told him," Stephanie hypothesized.

"I don't think so; it's hard to get an Islamic informant. He wouldn't give him up the first time he used him. There's something strange going on here, and I plan to get to the bottom of it."

"Is there anything else I can do?" asked Stephanie.

"No, sweetie. You did great, but that's all the risks I want you to take. These guys play for keeps. It's a certainty that they've killed before, and won't hesitate to do it again. You go back to work, and just keep your eyes and ears open for me."

"Will do," Stephanie said.

The next day, Thursday the thirteenth, Dan was back in his office. The morning had been taken up with meetings. Dan couldn't verify the info he had on Brad from Hamilton's list until just now. He was looking at a picture of his old friend on the computer screen. It was Brad's old army ID picture that came up when he entered the SSN from Hamilton's list. It was Brad all right that Hamilton was interested in. Dan looked at the time. It was 2 p.m.; Brad was probably still at work. Hamilton's info was complete. Dan knew all about Brad, his wife, and his father-in-law. He made a mental note to call Brad this evening.

Dan got home to his apartment around 6:00 p.m. He had supper, went to his sofa with a bottle of beer, and his cell phone. He dialed Brad's cell phone number. He couldn't trust the landline since Brad was on Hamilton's list.

"Hello?" a voice from the past answered.

Chapter Twelve

Brad read the date off of the morning paper he bought on the way to work, Monday, January 10, 2022. It's been almost a week since the funeral, and Brad still had trouble believing Dad was gone. Mary had taken an extra week leave of absence. She just couldn't face going to work yet. She stayed at home going through the boxes of effects from Dad's house. The day proved uneventful for Brad. He had a class this evening at the college, but was thinking of skipping it. He was concerned about leaving Mary alone at night so soon after Dad's death. A phone call to Mary soon put his concerns to rest. She assured him that she would be all right, and she didn't want him skipping any classes for her.

After class, Brad went directly home as fast as he could legally go. He unlocked the kitchen door, and was immediately greeted by Big Dog. Brad gave him a pat on the head and went into the living room to see Mary. The living room was scattered with various knickknacks, pictures, and mementoes from Dad's house. Mary was standing in the middle of the disarray looking a little lost.

Brad went to her, put an arm around her, and asked, "Are you OK?"

"Oh, yes, I'm fine. I just can't decide what I want to keep and what I want to give away, that's all."

"Well, nobody says you have to make a decision tonight."

Mary smiled and said, "You're right of course. I guess you could help me unpack these last two boxes though."

Brad said, "Of course. I'll take this one, and you take that one."

Brad started unpacking the box he had picked. He recognized the things from Dad's living room. He looked at each piece as he took it out of the box and visualized where it had been in the room. When he got to the bottom of the box he got a surprise.

"Mary, I thought all of Dad's electronic equipment was in boxes in the garage?"

"They are."

"Then what is this doing in a box from the living room?" Brad held up the probe Dad was using to look into the cable box.

"Oh, that was lying on top of the TV stand next to the cable box."

Brad thought to himself, *Beside the cable box? What was it doing there?* Brad examined their cable box thoughtfully. He looked at the probes cable, and then the ventilation holes in the cover. *No!* Brad said in his thoughts. *It couldn't be! Could it? 1984! Big Brother! Black box! That's it!*

He knew what Dad was killed for, and it was big; no, gigantic! It took all his willpower not to blurt out his discovery, but if he was right, and he did say it out loud, he would be signing their death warrants! Brad formulated a plan in his head. Tomorrow he would take the probe to work, and confirm his suspicions. After that, it would depend on what he found inside the cable box. After all, he did know what to look for.

The day-to-day calendar on the wall behind the supervisor's desk of the cable service read, Tuesday, January 11, 2022. Brad picked up his work orders and went to his assigned service van. After two hours of work, he decided to take a break. He parked in a fast food restaurant's parking lot, and went inside to use the restroom and get a cup of coffee. After returning to his van he climbed into the back, took the probe out of its carrying case, and turned it on. He grabbed one of the new cable boxes to probe. He knew the GPS was active, but he also knew the device that eavesdropped on people would be inactive; if there was such a device. The eavesdropping device couldn't function without being connected to the cable network. After only a few seconds, Brad found what he was looking for. It was a black box towards the right front of the circuit board plugged into a socket. He agreed totally with Dad: this thing was very suspicious. The only thing to do now was get an expert's opinion. Brad would have to wait until tomorrow, Wednesday, to go to Bill with his discovery. He would be in the vicinity of the college on that day. Anyone tracking the GPS in the cable boxes wouldn't get suspicious of his going to the college on his lunch hour.

Brad pulled into the college parking lot at lunchtime on Wednesday, January 12. He went to the administration office and found out that Bill had an hour break between classes.

Great, Brad thought, *now all I have to do is find him.*

He found bill in his classroom of all places. There are TV's and cable boxes in every classroom. Brad persuaded Bill to come outside to his truck on the pretext of taking him to lunch. As soon as they were in the van, Brad told Bill all about his suspicions concerning Dad's death. He played the message Dad left on his cell phone, and then told Bill about what he had found in the cable box.

"I take it we aren't really going to lunch, are we?" Bill asked.

"No, I couldn't risk telling you in the classroom. If this is true, then anywhere a television and cable box is installed isn't safe."

"What's 1984 and Big Brother mean?"

"It refers to an old book written by George Orwell in 1948, entitled *1984*, and made into a movie in 1984. It's about a totalitarian form of government, where everyone is monitored by the government through their TV sets. The catch phrase of the movie is, 'Big Brother is watching.'"

"And you think that's what's going on here, and Paul was killed because he found out about it."

"Yes."

"Brad, I sure hope to hell you're wrong!"

"Me too, but I don't think I am."

"OK, let me see what you saw."

Bill looked at the screen of the probes monitor with disbelief.

"I can tell you one thing just by looking at the thing. It has nothing to do with the cable box's function as a cable box. It seems to have its own circuitry leading to the cable in port. Can we take it out of the box?" Bill asked.

"Yes, the GPS is separate, and is the only thing that is active at this time."

They removed the cable box cover, and then pulled the black box from its socket. Back in the college electronics lab, which was thankfully empty, Bill plugged the black box into a socket connected to an analytical computer. When the data came up on the screen they were careful not to say anything out loud. Bill had the computer print out the data, and they went back to Brad's van to read it.

Back in the van, Bill read the computer printout.

"Those bastards!" Bill said out loud.

"I take it Dad was right?"

"Those no-good spying sons of bitches."

"I'll take that as a yes," Brad said.

"This is one sophisticated piece of surveillance apparatus! This thing has eight micro parabolic microphones arranged in a circle with one in the middle. There is an array of these microphones on each surface of the cube; except the bottom."

"Wait a minute, Bill. Parabolic mikes are directional. How could they work in this application?"

"They're spread out, and angled so they have every area within their range covered."

"By the way, what is their range?" asked Brad.

"Well that's the good news; not very far. Their range is limited by their size; no more than a hundred feet in all directions. After that, the spread in the pattern is too great to be very affective."

"How's this thing transmitting? I know that fiber optic cables like the ones cable TV stations are using at present have an available band width of zero to nine hundred gigahertz. With MPEG compression ten channels are available per six MHZ of bandwidth. That makes fifteen hundred channels presently available to the customer, and all of those channels are being used."

"I know that too," Bill confirmed, "so my best guess, judging from this data, would be spread spectrum multiplexing."

"Isn't that used by satellite communications, and cellular phone networks?"

"I'm proud of you, Brad, you've been doing your homework. Yes it is. The signal is encoded and transmitted over the whole bandwidth. The use of a code makes the signal inherently secure. The receiver must know the code to un-spread the spectrum, and recover the signal."

"Wow! I guess that's why they pay you the big bucks, huh?"

"Yeah right, big bucks," Bill responded sarcastically.

"So what's receiving all these signals from millions of cable boxes; some kind of super computer?" asked Brad.

"No, I don't think so. They'd need a computer the size of New Jersey, and that would be a little bit hard to hide. I'm thinking a network of servers and databases in strategic places all over the United States. Probably in those servers they installed in the cable offices. The cable offices would be the ideal locations; they're all tied together because of the early warning system. The computers are probably programmed to listen for key words, then give an alert of some kind when the word is recognized. The word is stored in a database along with the time, date, and some kind of address. They probably use the phone number of the suspect residence to save database space.

"It really makes my flesh crawl to think some stranger could have been listening to personal conversations between Keesha and me!" Bill said angrily.

"You said a computer listens for key words."

"Come on, Brad, you were a computer tech in the Army; you know that no system is closed to humans. Someone with the right screen name and password always has access to the system."

"Yeah, I know, I was just thinking the same thing you were about the conversations, and doing some wishful thinking. Hell, I've got a box in our bedroom for crying out loud!"

"That doesn't matter actually, the one in your living room has more than enough range to cover your bedroom."

Now it was Brad's turn to be sarcastic. "Oh thanks a lot, that makes me feel so much better!"

"My question to you, Brad my man, is what do you intend to do with this information?"

"I don't know yet. I have to be careful; we don't know how high this conspiracy goes or who's involved. Hell, the president himself could be involved, although I rather doubt it. I think the DHS is behind this; it sounds like their brand of paranoia. I do know someone high up in the FBI, he's an old army buddy of mine, and a real straight arrow; I could give him a call."

"If you do, make sure you use your cell phone, and you're not near any cable boxes. It's a sure bet that 'black box' is the top-priority phrase for the computers to pick up on."

"I hear ya," Brad agreed.

"Now, we have a dilemma to address," stated Brad.

"What's that?"

"Do we, or do we not, tell our respective wives about this?"

"I don't see how we can't tell them."

"Yeah, I know. I was just hoping in your great wisdom you could come up with a profound reason for not telling them."

"Here's what my great wisdom is telling me. The good Lord have mercy on my soul if she finds out I knew about this and didn't tell her!" Bill said with great dread.

"Once again you have shown me the way of light and truth, and saved me from a fate too horrible to mention. I thank you," Brad said thankfully. "Let me out of here, my next class starts in five minutes. Just keep me informed, OK?"

"I sure will."

On the way home that night Brad called Mary and asked her to meet him outside the house when he got home. He said he wanted to take a ride and show her something. Of course he didn't want to show her anything; he just wanted to tell her about the cable boxes, and the real reason Dad died. After telling Mary the whole story, Brad was extremely impressed with her reaction. Oh, she was angry all right, but it was a controlled anger. She wanted to be a part of any and all actions Brad would be taking in bringing these animals to justice. Brad promised her that he would keep her in the loop right up to the end. When they got home that night the house wasn't home anymore. They had to watch every word they said, because the cable box was listening. Brad promised Mary it wouldn't be for very long.

Brad and Mary were watching a documentary on the Arctic and global warming when his cell phone rang.

Brad answered, "Hello?"

"Hey, Brad. It's Dan Crenshaw!"

"Dan? I was just about to call you!"

"No kidding? Wow, great minds do work alike."

Just then the cable box caught Brad's eye.

"Hey, Dan, hold on just a second, and I'll be right with you, OK?"

"Yeah sure, no problem."

Brad wrote on a piece of paper and gave it to Mary. The paper read, "it's FBI Agent Dan Crenshaw." Mary acknowledged the note and gave him the OK sign. Brad went outside a distance of around 150 feet from his house, and figured it was safe to talk. After exchanging pleasantries and figuring out how long it's been since they last saw each other, Dan stated the reason for his call. Dan said that he had something important to show Brad, and that he would rather do it in person, so they could talk about it. Then Brad said basically the same thing. Dan said he was catching a flight tomorrow after work, and would get in about 11:00 p.m. Over Dan's protests, Brad insisted he would pick Dan up at the airport and bring him home to stay with them. Dan finally agreed and said he was looking forward to seeing Brad and meeting Mary.

Thursday, January 13 went uneventfully. Brad got home at around 6 p.m., and then he and Mary went out for a veggie burger at their favorite health food restaurant. They didn't feel like staying home and not being able to talk freely. Of course they couldn't talk freely in the restaurant either, because all public facilities had cable boxes and TVs. At least in a public place there were a lot of conversations going on, and hopefully it was harder for the computer to pick out key words. They still watched their choice of words just in case they were wrong. The only place they felt the slightest freedom to talk was in the SUV. After dinner, they took in a movie. The movie let out at 10:30, so they decided to head out to the airport and wait for Dan's plane to get in.

Dan's plane was on time, and they met him at the debarking area. Brad introduced Mary, and they all headed to the luggage pickup. After retrieving Dan's luggage, they headed for the parking lot and Mary's SUV. Once in the SUV, Brad drove towards home, but made a detour into a Kmart parking lot. Brad stopped the SUV about as far away from the store as possible. Dan asked them why they were stopping. Brad related his story about Mary's father and what they found out about the cable boxes. Then Dan showed Brad the list from Hamilton's file, and all the pieces of the puzzle came together.

"So, Dan, what do we do about this, or maybe more appropriately, what can we do about this?" Brad asked.

"What do we do? I don't know, I'll need some time to think about it. What can we do? I don't know that either, but I can tell you what we can't do. We can't turn Hamilton in to any authorities," Dan warned.

"Why not?" Mary and Brad said simultaneously.

"Because we don't know who he has on his payroll for one. Another reason is because of what you told me about the cable boxes. Someone could slip and say something incriminating. Then Hamilton would have the dirty dozen making evidence disappear faster than food at a picnic for a group of fat farm dropouts. This Professor Keats you told me about. Can we trust him?"

"I would trust him with my life, just like I would you," Brad stated. "OK, then that's a start. We're going to need an electronics expert if my plan is going to work."

"Plan? You have a plan already?"

"Not really a plan, more like an idea. I'll need some time to work it out. I assume I can do that at your house?" asked Dan.

"Absolutely. Anything you need just let us know, and we'll do our best to get it for you."

"Good. Tomorrow you can inform Keats about what's going on. Tell him to hang in there for another day until I get the details of my plan worked out. Then we'll have a meeting, and everybody will have a chance to give their input and their opinion. Now, I'm beat. Let's get this buggy moving, and head for the barn."

Brad started the engine, and they drove off for 1932 Oak Street.

Friday morning, January 14, dawned gloomy and foreboding like in an old horror film. The weather looked like it could do anything from thunderstorm to blizzard; all that was needed was the right temperature. Brad and Mary went off to work. They left Dan and Big Dog to work on his plan to nail Hamilton. Big Dog took a liking to Dan, and trusted him. Brad and Mary took that to be a good sign. Big Dog, even at his young age, was becoming a good judge of human character. Around 12 noon, Dan decided to take the dog out and make a couple phone calls.

He decided to call Stephanie first. When he thought of her name a sudden feeling of panic came over him. He remembered that they had the conversation about the contents of Hamilton's file in Stephanie's apartment. He knew DC was the first city to complete the installation of the cable boxes, and that was days before their meeting.

What if their conversation was recorded? Could Hamilton know that she helped him? If he did know, what would he do about it?

Dan tried to replay their conversation in his head.

What key words did they say to alert the monitoring computer? After a few minutes of deep concentration and recall, Dan came to the conclusion that they had said nothing to alert the damned thing. He also concluded that Hamilton was too preoccupied with arranging the arrest of the five patsies to be monitoring his secretary's apartment. Now there was another question, should he tell Stephanie about the eavesdropping cable boxes?

He decided not to. He was sure that she wouldn't tell anyone about the info she had acquired for him. He called Stephanie on her cell phone when he figured she'd be at lunch, and found out what he needed to know. Mainly, what days Hamilton worked late? She said that he always worked late on Wednesday and Friday nights until 11 p.m., you could set your clock by it. He thanked her and told her that in a couple of weeks everything would be made public, and Hamilton would get what he deserved. His next call went to Kelly in records, the girl he left in the lurch on New Year's Day.

"Hello?"

"Hi, Kelly. It's Dan."

"Oh hi, Dan. How are you?"

"I'm fine. How are you doing?"

"Great! Actually I owe you my sincere gratitude."

"How so?"

"Well after you left on New Year's Day, I went back to my apartment. When I got in there was a message on my answering machine; it was an old boyfriend of mine from college. Well, so as not to bore you with a long story, we met for coffee that day. Now two weeks later we're engaged to be married, and I couldn't be happier!"

"Wow! That's great, Kelly. I'm very happy for you!"

"Thank you, Dan. Now what can I do for you?"

"First, tell me where you are right now. I know that sounds strange, but you'll find out the reason I'm asking in a week or so."

"That's OK, Dan, I'm used to your strange questions. I'm in my car. I just got back from lunch."

"Good, can you get me a copy of the schematics for the servers that the government installed in the cable vision buildings?"

"Gee, Dan, I sure would like to, but they're under lock and key, and it takes special clearance to get at them."

"So there isn't any way I can get a copy?"

"I didn't say that. There's a copy in every installation site to expedite servicing. If you know an employee of a cable company he may be able to get you a copy. I'll bet they're not very careful about securing them."

"How about some floor plans?" Dan asked.

"That I can do. Just give me the addresses, and I'll send them out to you."

Dan told her the two addresses, and what he specifically needed.

"Thanks, Kelly. I owe you one."

"No thanks necessary, Dan. Bye."

"Bye, Kelly."

Dan couldn't help a distinct feeling of loss over the news Kelly just related to him. He didn't realize how close he had gotten to her over the years. He came to the realization that there was something missing in his life. He made a resolution that after this case was over, he would take time to smell the roses, so to speak. Maybe look up Stephanie and see where their relationship could lead, if he put it first. No time for that now though; the civil rights of the entire population of the United States was in jeopardy. It was time to go inside and finish the details of his plan. Tomorrow was Saturday, January 15; everyone would be off work and eager to hear what he had in mind.

Friday night was uneventful. Everyone just watched TV, and made small talk at the Spencer house. Brad and Dan were careful not to mention anything about their experiences in the gulf for fear of triggering an alert. Before they went to bed, Dan gave Brad a note asking him when and where they could have a meeting with Keats. Brad wrote back saying anytime he wanted. Dan wrote 10:00 a.m. Brad gave the OK sign and everybody went to bed.

Saturday morning, Dan was up early working out the final details of his plan. Brad and Mary were up getting breakfast and taking care of Big Dog. After breakfast Brad called Bill Keats and told him to be ready at 10 a.m. like Dan requested. At five minutes to 10 a.m. the trio climbed into the SUV and drove down the street to Bill's house. When they pulled into the drive there were two people waiting for them.

"Dan, this is Professor Bill Keats and his wife Keesha."

"A pleasure to finally meet you, sir. Brad speaks very highly of you."

"Nice to meet you too, Agent Crenshaw," Bill and Keesha said in turn.

"Keesha insisted on coming along. I hope that's OK?"

"Absolutely. My plan calls for five operatives. You've solved the last problem I was having with it."

Brad drove out of town towards a state park about ten miles out of town. The park was virtually deserted this time of year. Brad parked in the middle of a parking lot located on top of a small hill.

"Good choice, Brad," Dan said. "We can see someone coming for miles before they see us. Out here in the open we have 360-degree visibility no chance of anyone sneaking up on us. Glad to see you haven't forgotten your special ops training; you're going to need it."

Dan proceeded to explain his plan to his team. When he was through with his explanation, he asked for comments. Everyone agreed Dan's plan was bold and daring, but if it succeeded it would reveal Hamilton, his cronies, and the horrible infringement of everyone's civil rights to the world.

Next, Dan had a couple of questions for everyone. He wanted to know if they all knew how to use a firearm? They told him about their target shooting excursions and put his doubts to rest. Next he wanted to know if they could shoot a human being if it became necessary? They assured him, if it became necessary, they would be able to rise to the occasion.

Then Dan started handing out orders. "OK then, Brad, I want you, on Monday, to find out where the schematics for the servers are kept, and get a copy. Professor Keats?"

"Please call me Bill," Professor Keats insisted.

"OK, Bill, I want you to rig up some two-way radios with rotating frequencies. Rotating, so anyone picking up our conversation will not be able to tell what we're talking about, or triangulate us."

"How many frequencies?" Bill asked.

"At least five or six."

"OK, no problem."

"Next, after Brad gets a copy of the schematics, you have to buy the equipment we need for your part in the plan. I can get you started with this check for five thousand dollars made out to you. If you need more let me know; I don't have much of a social life so I have a sizable savings to tap," Dan explained.

"I think this should do nicely. Tomorrow I'll go shopping at the Electronics Outlet Store downtown. The store's open on Sunday, so I can get a jump on what we need. I really don't need the schematics to know what to buy; I just need them to know where to hook it up."

"Good," Dan said approvingly.

"What about weapons?" Brad asked.

"I know of an army surplus store in Cincinnati that's not quite legal and above board. Brad, you and I will go in like a couple of FBI agents, and threaten the owner with a federal rap. He just might be persuaded to outfit us with some equipment," Dan answered.

"What about the cable box in the store?" Brad asked.

"I don't think we'll have to use any key words for the box to hit on."

"When do we go?"

"Like Bill, we can get an early start and leave tomorrow morning."

"Sounds like a plan to me," Brad confirmed.

Sunday morning, January 16, 2022, saw Brad and Dan heading for Cincinnati at 6 a.m.. On the way, Dan told Brad the plan to trick the store owner. They got to the surplus store around 10:30 a.m. Brad went in according to the plan. He walked around the store looking at various items until the store was empty.

Then he approached the owner and said, "Hawk sent me. He says you're the guy that can fix me up with something special."

"That's a neat trick for Hawk, since he's been dead for a year," the store owner said.

Brad was unshaken; he knew that it was all part of a code.

"Hawk's not dead, soldiers of fortune never die, they just fade away," Brad replied.

The store owner looked Dan in the eye for a moment, and then smiled and said, "How is old Hawk anyway?"

Dan had warned him about an extra test. "Maybe I'm in the wrong store," Brad said and turned to leave.

"Hold on, guy, I was just testing you. What kind of something special were you looking for?"

"I need a suppressed MP five with two extra clips, and plenty ammo."

"Jesus, what are you going to do, rob a bank?"

Brad grabbed a bayonet from the counter top behind the store owner. With one motion he had the scabbard off, and the bayonet at the man's throat.

"You ask too many fucking questions, man! Too many questions can get a man killed!"

"OK, OK! I get your point," the store owner said. Feeling the tip of the bayonet at his jugular vein he said, "I get it in more ways than one!"

Brad put the scabbard back on the bayonet. The store owner locked the front door and led Brad to the back of the store. He unlocked a display case and turned a display knife counterclockwise. A perfectly camouflaged door swung open, and a secret room was revealed. Brad could hardly believe his eyes as he stepped through the doorway. There was enough weapons and ammunition to equip a company of Army Rangers. Most of the weapons were illegal to own or have in your possession.

Just then they both heard movement behind them, and they both turned around at the same time. "How the hell did you get in here!" the store owner asked.

"FBI," Dan said as he raised his seven-millimeter Glock in one hand and his ID in the other. "Don't worry, I locked the door behind me, so we won't be interrupted."

"I suppose you're with him?" the store owner asked Brad.

Brad smiled and said, "You're a smart man; now let's see how smart you can be. We're on a mission to save the civil rights of every man, woman, and child in these United States, including the right to bear arms."

The store owner turned to Dan and asked, "Is he for real?"

"Yep."

"Let me see that ID again?"

Dan gave the man his ID to study up close. "It's real all right. What do you guys need?"

Dan gave the store owner a list: five Kevlar vests, five suppressed MP fives, twenty-four clips, six flash-bang grenades, three Tasers and two cases of ammunition.

"How much?" Dan asked looking over the boxes of weapons and equipment on the counter.

"Seeing how you guys are defending my constitutional rights, I'll give it all to you at cost, four thousand bucks."

"Sounds fair to me." Dan pulled an envelope out of his pocket, counted out four thousand dollars, and handed it to the store owner.

As the man grabbed the money, Dan held on to it, and gave him a warning. "We were never here; understood? If I hear that you so much as told your mother's cat what went on here today, you'll spend so much time in a federal prison, you'll think gray is the only color on earth. Got it?"

"Yes, but my mother doesn't have a cat."

"Exactly," said Dan as he and Brad carried the boxes of equipment out to the SUV.

They covered the weapons and equipment with a couple of blankets and headed for home. On the way home they stopped at a sporting goods store, and bought five paintball guns including ammunition.

Brad and Dan arrived home about 5:30 p.m. They left the equipment and weapons in the SUV and went into the house. As they entered, they gave Mary and Big Dog a benign greeting supplemented by an OK sign, signifying every thing went well. Dan wrote on one of the pads they had placed around the house in strategic areas, and handed it to Brad. Brad read the note and went out to make a call to Bill. When Bill answered, Brad asked how his grocery shopping went? Bill said it went well, actually better than expected, and he was checking them out when he called. Brad told Bill that their shopping went well also, and that the plan was going forward. Brad then reported to Dan that everything went well with Bill also.

Tomorrow Brad would get a copy of the schematics Bill needed, and take an emergency leave of absence for two weeks. Bill, Keesha, and Mary would call their place of employment and either report off, or get an emergency leave of absence for some reason or another. Dan would just cash in on some of the huge amount of vacation days he had accumulated over the years. By Tuesday morning, Mary, Brad, and Dan would be on their way to Dad's farm. Keesha and Bill would be joining them after Bill finished his electronics work.

Monday morning, January 17, Brad went to work as usual. He applied for and got a two-week leave of absence starting the next day. Then he went about his usual workday. At the end of the day, Brad stayed behind on the pretense of filling out some paperwork before his leave of absence started. Once he was alone, and before the security guard came on duty, he had a chance to look for the schematics. It wasn't much of a search; he found them in the second drawer he looked in. The schematics were in a three-ring binder, so it was easy to make a copy of them at the copying machine. He put the binder back in the drawer where he found it. As he was leaving the security guard was coming on duty. The guard said good night to Brad and Brad returned the salutation. On the way home Brad dropped off the copies of the schematics at Bill's house. Then he continued up the street to home.

Tuesday morning, January 18, was a sloppy morning. It was just cold enough to snow, but not quite cold enough to accumulate rapidly, resulting in slush. Dan, Brad, Mary, and Big Dog loaded into the SUV and headed for Dads farm. When they arrived at the farm Mary and Brad realized it was the first time they had been there since the funeral. It was an emotional time for them, but they knew they had to suck it up and concentrate on the plan. The rest of the day was spent in the barn. They made an effective training course using the scrap lumber and sheets of plywood Dad had stored in the barn. In one corner of the barn they set up a training area for hand-to-hand combat. In the woods against a hill, they set up a target range to practice loading and firing the MP fives. This was a serious and dangerous mission they were undertaking. Making it even more dangerous was the fact that three out of the five team members have had no formal combat training. Even Brad admitted that he was a little rusty and needed a refresher course. Since Brad had been a computer tech, and only cross-trained in special ops, he had no actual combat experience. Dan was the only one with combat experience, and would be everyone's instructor.

They decided to stay in Dad's house even though the cable box was still hooked up in compliance with the law. No one new they were there, and the farm wasn't on the market yet, so no realtor would be coming around with potential buyers. The neighbors knew Mary's SUV from before, and probably would assume she was there fixing up the place for sale. For beds, they brought sleeping bags and inflatable air mattresses. It was late after they completed their setup, so they decided to go right to bed after supper. Tomorrow the training would start.

Wednesday morning, January 18, was cold and snowing. The slush had turned to ice overnight, and there was an inch of snow on the ground. Dan started his two assault team members with a lesson in the cold barn. The first lesson was on the MP five.

Dan started out by saying, "The MP five is a handheld compact machine gun. It has a selector switch which gives the shooter a choice of fully automatic, a burst of three rounds, or single round semi-auto. I won't be going into things like rate of fire and the like. You don't need to know those details to load the weapon and pull the trigger. Now, I'll show you how to break the weapon down, clean it, and reassemble it. That you do need to know."

Dan proceeded to demonstrate the proper technique to disassemble the weapon and clean it. Then he demonstrated how to reassemble the weapon, insert a clip, and prepare to fire. Brad and Mary practiced the technique for over an hour until their fingers were so cold they ceased to function. Dan gave them a break so they could put on their gloves and warm their hands. Dan's next task was to put his two trainees through the obstacle course. The obstacle course was set up to look like the inside of an office with desks, chairs, tables and filing cabinets. Dan put them through different scenarios. He taught them how take cover and return fire. He had them assault and overrun fake enemy positions over and over again. They practiced firing from cover with the paintball guns. If they exposed too much of themselves, Dan was only too happy to nail the exposed body part with a shot from his paintball gun. They broke for lunch at 1 p.m. After lunch, Dan drilled them on his plan, and asked them to recite it back in turn. He made it clear that all members of the team should know the plan backwards and forwards.

Dan could not make it clear enough that this was not a game. There was the very real possibility of going up against twelve experienced ex-CIA operatives. If they weren't properly trained, the team could be taken out before they even got started. Later on, they went to the target range where they practiced firing the MP five from all possible positions in burst, semi-auto, and fully automatic mode. A two-mile run topped off their first training day. When they returned to Dad's house they were feeling the effects of their first day of training; tired and sore.

Thursday morning, January 20, was even colder than the day before. The training was even more intense than on Wednesday, and more physically demanding. Brad and Mary showed Dan that they were more than up for it. The couple was gaining more and more of Dan's respect as each hour went by. After all, they were going after the killers of Paul Lorinsky; there was no higher motivation for them than that. In the evening, Bill and Keesha arrived. Bill had completed the electronics work and had all the equipment they needed to get the job done. The next morning they would start the same training that Mary and Brad had been going through for the past two days. They would learn to work as a team, each one of them covering the other, and responsible for the other's life. Like the fingers and thumb of a hand each one working together to make a fist.

Saturday, January 22, was cold and gloomy, but no one let it dampen his or her spirits. Training went forward as scheduled; everyone was starting to get toughened up, and dedicated to completing the mission.

At the end of the day in the barn, Dan evaluated their performance and told each of them where they needed work. "Overall, I think you guys are doing incredibly well, and I'm proud to be working with you. Now, tomorrow morning we will be…"

"Uh, Dan?" Brad interrupted. "Sorry to interrupt, but tomorrow morning is Sunday, and the four of us were planning to go to church. You're doing a fantastic job preparing us physically, but the four of us need to prepare spiritually also. You're welcome to come with us of course."

Dan thought for a minute. He hadn't been to church for quite a long time; maybe too long. It sure couldn't hurt to have God on their side. "Yes, of course, I'll go with you."

After supper, everyone went to their respective rooms and prepared for bed. Bill and Keesha had a bath to themselves, and likewise did Brad and Mary. Dan used Brad and Mary's shower to clean up and then went up to his room for the night. Brad was sitting on the edge of their air mattress bed with his tired head hanging down.

"Hey, sweetie, I'm going to take a shower," Mary said.

"OK," Brad said without raising his head.

"Care to join me?"

Brad looked toward the direction Mary's voice came from. Mary was framed in the doorway of the bathroom wearing nothing but a bath towel, a small bath towel at that! Her beautiful golden brown hair flowed down just over her shoulders, and her skin was aglow from the cold day they had spent training outside. Her brown eyes were dark and inviting as were her pink lips. Her beautiful long legs were displayed to their fullest potential without being overly revealing.

Brad thought, *A man would have to be a eunuch or gay not to accept her invitation!*

Brad, being neither a eunuch nor gay, couldn't get his clothes off fast enough. They got into the shower, and after washing each other they made beautiful love together. The warm sensation of the water flowing over them heightened and magnified the pleasure of their lovemaking bringing both of them to a climactic conclusion! After drying off, they put on their sleeping clothes and got into bed. They hadn't made love since before finding out about the cable boxes. Neither Brad nor Mary wanted to entertain some government agent with their sex life. Sleep overtook them almost immediately, and they slept like a rock until the alarm went of at 8:30 a.m.

Sunday morning, January 23, 10 a.m., found Brad, Mary, Keesha, Bill, and Dan heading for church in the SUV. After the church service, everyone was standing in line to shake hands with Reverend Woodward. While Dan was waiting, he thought about the service and the way he was feeling at present. He had been to church services before, and quite frankly he had been happy to leave when they were over. This time was different; he couldn't quite put his finger on it. Maybe it was Reverend Woodward's stile of preaching, or the atmosphere of peace and love that prevailed over the service. Whatever it was, Dan felt strangely empowered. He knew they were doing the right thing, and he also knew that his plan, if given a chance, would work. When it was the five friends' turn to compliment the reverend, Brad introduced Dan, Keesha, and Bill. The Reverend Woodward shook their hands and quickly said to all of them, "You're all on the Lord's mission, and he will be with you to the end."

At the bottom of the steps after receiving Reverend Woodward's words of encouragement, one of Dad's neighbors approached to say hello.

"Hi. I'm Chad Livingston."

"Yes, Mr. Livingston, I remember you from Dad's funeral. How are you?" asked Mary.

"Oh I'm fine, and please, call me Chad."

"OK, how can I help you, Chad?"

" Oh, I don't need any help, but I thought you might."

"In what way, Chad?"

"Well, I was passing by your father's place the other day, and noticed you were working in the barn. I said to myself, self, I'd bet it's mighty cold in that barn for those people. Then I remembered that old kerosene torpedo heater I had just sit'n around collectin' dust. Sumthin told me you'd be at church this morn'n, so I brought it in the back of my pickup."

"Well thank you, Chad, that's very kind of you, we sure could use it," Mary said thankfully.

They loaded the heater into the SUV, and the five gallons of kerosene that Chad had been thoughtful enough to bring. They thanked him repeatedly, and promised to return it as soon as they were through with it. Then they got into the SUV and headed for the farm.

On the way back to the farm, Dan had a question for Brad. "You didn't tell Reverend Woodward about our mission, did you, Brad?"

"No, definitely not. You know I wouldn't talk to anyone about that, and neither did Mary, I'm sure."

"Then how did he know we're on any mission at all?"

"Probably the same way he knew to tell me a while back that I would be finishing the work that Dad had started."

"How's that?" Dan asked.

"The Lord told him. Who else?" Brad answered.

Then Mary, Bill, and Keesha said, "Amen."

"Gee, I guess that would mean that God is on our side, huh?" Dan asked.

"Looks like it to me," Bill said.

"I know one thing for sure. He wants us to be warm from now on," Keesha added.

Everybody agreed and laughed gratefully.

Sunday afternoon they fired up the heater in the barn, and everybody learned how to use a Taser; especially Keesha. The ability to use a Taser was crucial to Keesha's part of the plan. Then came training on the radios that Bill had ingeniously modified. The radios rotated frequencies in perfect synchronization with one another. Then Dan demonstrated the proper use of a flash-bang grenade. Dan cut the training short then, and gave everyone the rest of the evening off to rest. They were going to need rest because the next three days would be the toughest of their lives.

The next three days, January 24, 25, and 26, were straight from hell. They trained sixteen hours a day with only fifteen minutes apiece for breakfast and lunch. They did everything with full equipment over and over again until they could do it in their sleep. They studied satellite and virtual pictures of the target buildings until their eyes refused to focus. They knew the floor plan of Hennery's office building better than the floor plan of their respective homes.

On Wednesday evening, January 26, after training hard all day, Dan announced what everyone had been waiting to hear.

"There's nothing more I can teach you about this mission, or to prepare you for it. So tomorrow morning at 10 a.m., we will load up our gear and head for Washington, DC. It should take around eight hours to get there doing the speed limit. The last thing we want is some gung-ho highway patrolman stopping us and getting suspicious. I've made reservations at a motel close to the target building. Keesha, you will take the SUV to your target as planned. Do you have your mission down, and are you sure of the route?"

"You have got to be kidding! After the last three days, I could do it in my sleep!" Keesha answered.

"Bill, do you have your uniform for your little covert operation on Friday morning?"

"Sure do, boss, and all the equipment I need to plant in the room."

"What if Hamilton decides to have the offices swept after you leave?"

"They can't detect any transmitters if they're not active. That's what these ballpoint pens are for. Each of you carries one. When you get into Hamilton's outer offices click the pen once to activate the devices. Once they activate them, the pens will have no further effect on the devices."

"Brad and Mary, are you ready for the assault, and do you know your parts?"

"Dan, I think I can speak for both of us when I say, I have never been more ready for anything in my life," Brad answered.

"OK. On the way tomorrow, I will give you copies of the pictures I have of the Dirty Dozen. You can study them on the way to Washington. Any questions?"

"Yes, I have one, but it's not for you, Dan, it's for Bill."

"Ask away, Brad," Bill said.

"Bill, you said there's probably about two hundred of these servers and databases strategically placed in cable offices all over the country. Right?"

"Yes."

"Even with computers listening there has to be hundreds of thousands of hits on key words. Hamilton couldn't possibly be sorting them out himself, could he?"

"No, he would need at least one person in each location to sort through all the hits and decide what's valid and what isn't."

"Then my next question is to you, Dan. How does he keep around two hundred or more people loyal to him without one of them getting cold feet?" Brad asked.

"LD 37."

"What?!" Everyone asked together.

Dan repeated himself, "LD 37. The LD stands for loyalty drug. It's derived from a tropical plant that grows in South America. Do you remember the so-called mind-expanding drug that became popular in the seventies, called LSD?" Everyone nodded yes. "LSD had a strange property; it didn't leave the body after the effects wore off. LSD was stored in the brain, and every so often was released giving the former user flashbacks. These flashbacks could keep recurring all through the ex-user's life. LD 37 is like LSD; it's stored in the brain, but instead of hallucinations it makes the user extremely loyal to whomever is his superior. Whenever the user gets doubts about his superior the drug is released, and the user is fiercely loyal again. Ancient native South American tribal leaders used this plant to keep their warriors loyal to them.

"There was some talk about inoculating the members of the armed forces with the drug. But the plant is extremely rare and difficult to grow in a greenhouse. Also scientists as of yet have failed to synthesize the chemical composition of the plant's derivative. If they ever synthesize the drug, there's no telling what they'll do with it. It has one other grave weakness. The drug can't be stored for more than seventy-two hours; even if it's refrigerated it goes sour. So it can't be stored in great quantities yet either. I found out about it by accident. I was sent an email by mistake telling me the whole story. I checked out the email, and it was valid. Someone had made a typo, and mailed it to me."

"Is there an antidote?" Keesha asked.

"The email didn't say."

"Man, that's some story! Right out of the science fiction books; only it's reality!" Bill said. Everyone else agreed.

"Any more questions? Then I just want to say one more thing. It has been a privilege and an honor to be your instructor this past week. I have never seen a more dedicated or tougher group of trainees in my entire career. I want you to know that whatever happens, you will always have my highest respect. OK, let's get cleaned up and get something to eat."

Thursday morning, January 27, 2022, 10 a.m., the SUV fully loaded with six occupants and their equipment pulled out of the farmhouse's driveway. First stop was the neighbor that took care of Big Dog during the funeral. They said that they would be happy to take care of him for a couple of days until they got back. Next, they dropped off the borrowed torpedo heater at Chad's farm with a full five-gallon can of kerosene. Then they were on their way to Washington to fulfill their destiny.

Chapter Thirteen

Wednesday, January 12, 2022, Hennery Hamilton read from the top of the paper he had picked up on his way to work. "Terrorist Cell Busted: Suspects Believed Guilty of Bombings!"

"Now that's what I call a headline," Hennery said to himself.

He looked at his computer monitor and noted all the congratulatory emails. Information is power, maybe the greatest power of all, and he had exclusive access to it. This bust was an important step. He would soon be manipulating his way to the position of director of the DHS. Then, from director of the DHS to the presidency. Yes, sir, the information highway was going to be his yellow brick road, that was certain. The rest of the day was spent receiving kudos from just about everyone, even the president himself.

Thursday, January 13, Hennery sat in the soundproof glass cubicle that was his office, and surveyed the outer office. He liked the idea of the glass partitions because he could keep tabs on his employees, but they couldn't eavesdrop on him. Also, if someone was headed for his door he could put sensitive materials away before they got there. Hennery took out his keys and unlocked the lower right-hand drawer of his desk. He took out the one folder that he kept in it and laid it on his desktop. Hennery opened the folder and took out the sheet of paper with the personal info about the five terrorist suspects. He was about to go to his copy machine with the sheet of paper, when he noticed a very faint smudge at the top. It was a peculiar smudge. It wasn't dirt; it was kind of flesh colored. He didn't remember it being there when he put the paper away last time.

Had someone been in the drawer snooping, and if so, who? Hennery wondered.

166

Hennery went to his copy machine and made five copies of the list of personal info. He went back to his desk, took out five envelopes, and put each of the terrorist's names on an envelope. Then he put a copy of the list in each envelope and sealed it. He then called one of the guards on his payroll at the secret prison where the suspects were being held. He told the guard that the envelopes would be delivered to him this afternoon. Hennery had to make sure that each suspect would get an envelope on his dinner tray that evening. He then called Zeke, of the dirty dozen, to come and pick up the envelopes, and to deliver them to the guard. It took Zeke about forty-five minutes to get there. After he left, Hennery made another phone call to another member of the dirty dozen.

"Hello, Harry?"

"Yes, sir."

"Harry, I see from your bio that you have extensive training in forensics."

"Yes, sir, I do."

"Id like you to come to my office tomorrow first thing in the morning, I have an important job for you."

"Yes, sir. What time, sir?"

"Oh, let's say 8 a.m.."

"You got it, sir, 8 a.m. it is."

After hanging up, Hennery put the list with the smudge on it into a plastic protective sleeve, and locked it in his briefcase. He was making sure that whoever got into his drawer, if someone did get into his drawer, wouldn't be walking off with the evidence.

Friday, January 14, 8 a.m., Hennery looked up from his desk and saw Harry making his way to his door. Hennery waved at Harry to come in.

"Harry, glad to see you; sit down."

"Thank you, sir. How are you, sir?"

"Fine, fine."

Hennery was looking through his briefcase for the sheet of paper in the plastic sleeve.

"Ah, here it is," he said, pulling the plastic sleeve and its contents from the briefcase.

He handed the package to Harry. "You see that smudge at the top of that sheet of paper?"

Harry examined the top of the paper and replied, "Yes, sir."

"First of all, I want you to identify that substance. Then I want you to check the paper for prints," Hennery ordered.

"Yes, sir."

Harry was looking at the smudge with a pocket magnifying glass. "I can't be certain until I look at it under a microscope, but my best guess would be makeup, sir."

"Well, make sure, Harry. I need to know for certain."

"You got it, sir. Sir, I'm going to need a lab."

"I'll get you clearance to use one of the NSA's labs. I'll let you know which one later on today. Harry, whatever you do, do not let anyone see what's written on that piece of paper; understand?"

"Yes, sir, I understand completely."

Hennery spent the rest of the day setting up some terrorist suspects for future arrests. He also worked on a plan to kidnap the secretary of defense sometime in the future. He wasn't the least bit concerned about someone discovering the plans. If they did, he would just say he was working out worst-case scenarios. He called the NSA, and arranged for Harry to use one of their labs alone. He then called Harry, told him were to go, and who to talk to. He told him this was his work-late night, and to call him either tonight, or in the morning if he found anything out.

Saturday morning, 8:30 a.m., Hennery woke up to his cell phone ringing. He looked at the caller ID; it was Harry. Hennery took the phone off the charger, answered, and told Harry to hold. Then he went downstairs into his study and took a seat at his desk.

"OK, Harry, what have you got for me?"

"First of all, sir, I'm sorry, but I couldn't get finished until after you had left the office last night. After I give you my results you'll see why."

"That's OK, lay it on me."

"The smudge was makeup. According to the charts the manufacturer is Avon. The type of woman wearing it would be between the ages of thirty and forty, Caucasian, her complexion is a little on the dark side, maybe half Italian, half English, or Scottish.

"I dusted and tried chemicals to raise prints, but I came up empty except for yours of course. Next I used forensic tape to pull any trace substances off of the paper. I found white powder, sir."

"White powder?"

"Yes, sir, like the kind rubber surgical gloves have on the inside to make them go on easier."

"So, that proves someone has been looking at that paper with gloves on so as not to leave fingerprints."

"Yes, sir, I'm afraid it does, but instead of fingerprints they left something much better behind."

"What's that?"

"I was able to get several epithelial cells from the smudge on the paper. I extracted the DNA from them, and printed out the profile. That's what took me so long, I didn't finish until 3 a.m. this morning. You know, sir, if I may make a suggestion here?"

"Go ahead."

"I would look close to home for the suspect. Someone who has easy access to your office, wouldn't look out of place in it, and knows your routine. When you come up with a suspect, try and get a DNA sample, and I can see if it matches."

"Thanks for your confirmation, Harry, I was thinking along those lines myself. Harry, you did excellent work, and you've earned a ten-thousand-dollar bonus."

"The pleasure was all mine, sir, and thank you for the bonus."

Hennery hung up his cell phone and started thinking. After a few minutes only one suspect kept coming to the forefront, Stephanie. She had a key to his office, wouldn't look out of place if someone saw her in there, and she definitely knew his routine.

"What was her last name anyway?"

He kept a list of employees' names, phone numbers and addresses in his desk. He brought up Stephanie's phone number on his cell phone to match to hers on the list. When he got to the M's he found her, Stephanie Mackenzie.

"Definitely Scottish, and I bet her mother was Italian," Hennery speculated.

Now he wondered about something else. She had a key to his office, but not to his desk drawer. He would have definitely noticed if the drawer was jimmied or pried open in any way. He would have to look into Stephanie's full background Monday, and see what he could find out.

Monday morning, January 17, bright and early Hennery made his way through the outer office to the glass cubicle that was his office. No one was in yet. He sat down behind his desk, set the coffee down that he had bought on the way to work along with the paper, and turned on his computer. As the computer booted up he read the headlines on the paper, "Terrorist Suspects Confess!"

"Ah the power of information when used properly or improperly." Hennery wasn't quite sure which term applied in this case.

He knew that those boys would rather confess and go to jail than disgrace their families. Disgraced not only in this country, but their extended families back in Iraq would be disgraced too. Now they were blooming heroes.

"Hell, I did them a fucking favor when you come to think about it," Hennery said out loud.

Hennery's computer had finished booting, and it took him about two seconds to get into the employee database search screen. He typed in Stephanie Mackenzie, and her file came up with everything anyone needed to know about her.

"Father's name, James Mackenzie; mother's name, Maria Napolitano; Italian, big surprise," Hennery said under his breath.

He scrolled down through the info until he got to father's occupation.

170

"Well, I'll be damned." There, across from the category "occupation," was typed in, "Locksmith."

"I'll bet just like the ideal father, Mr. Mackenzie taught his daughter a thing or two about picking locks," Hennery said sarcastically.

He was building quite a case against Ms. Mackenzie; all he needed was a sample of her DNA to make it conclusive. It was 9 a.m. and everyone was heading off the elevator, and to his or her workstations. Stephanie was the fourth person to get off the elevator and head for her desk. Hennery watched her put her purse beside her desk and head over to the coffee machine. Then, she walked back to her desk, put the coffee down, and came his way. Hennery pretended to be reading the paper when she knocked. He looked up and motioned her in.

"Anything I can do for you this morning, Mr. Hamilton?"

"No, Stephanie, I think I have everything under control this morning, thank you," is what he said. What he really wanted to say was, "Yes, I would like a sample of your DNA please."

He knew that it would be only a matter of time before he got the sample he needed. The opportunity to get a sample of Stephanie's DNA presented itself that afternoon. Hennery was at his desk doing some paperwork and watching Stephanie out of the corner of his eye. She decided to take a break at her desk and have a cup of yogurt from the vending machine. She finished the yogurt and cleaned the plastic spoon off like everybody else. She put the spoon in her mouth and pulled it out over her tongue and between her lips.

Hennery watched and said quietly to himself, "There must be a thousand epithelial cells on that spoon."

He watched as she put the spoon in the empty plastic cup, and dropped it in her wastebasket. Hennery called Stephanie into his office and handed her an envelope he had been saving for just this reason. He told her to take it to the mailroom personally and get a receipt for it. Not an unusual request; he asks her to do it about three or four times a week. After she left, it was a simple matter to walk over to her desk and pretend to be looking for something. Then he accidentally dropped a paper into her wastebasket, and while retrieving it, took the spoon out. Back at his desk he carefully dropped the spoon into a plastic bag and zipped it shut.

"Hello, Harry?"

"Yes, sir."

"I got that DNA sample for you. Come by and pick it up," Hennery ordered.

"Yes, sir. I'll have the results for you by morning."

"Good,"

Hennery hung up his cell phone and leaned back in his chair. *Well, Stephanie, we will soon know if it was you, won't we? Then there will be another question to answer, won't there? It's a sure bet that you didn't just all of a sudden get curious. You're working for someone, and I need to find out who it is as soon as possible.*

Tuesday morning, January 18, Hennery got to his office around 9 a.m.. He no sooner sat down behind his desk than his cell phone rang.

"Hello?"

"Hello, sir. It's Harry."

"Yes, Harry, what have you got for me?"

"A ninety-eight percent match. They don't get any closer than that, sir."

"Thank you, Harry. I thought it would be."

"You're welcome, sir. Goodbye."

"Yes, goodbye, Harry."

Now he knew beyond a shadow of a doubt that Stephanie was the spy. Next he had to find out who she was working for. Hennery took out the folder of the Dirty Dozen and looked through the pictures of each man. He stopped when he got to Tom. He looked at the picture carefully. Tom is a handsome, well-built athletic type, with an Ivy League education. "Yes, he will do very nicely."

Hennery called Stephanie into his office at 2:00 p.m.

"Stephanie, I'd like to ask a favor of you. There's a high-ranking officer from Canada's Royal Mounted Police visiting us to observe how our NSA SWAT teams train. He's single, and he's been here for a couple of days all alone. The director DHS would like someone to take him around to dinner, and maybe a couple of shows. You know, show him some good old American hospitality. Please don't get the wrong idea though; this is completely on a platonic level. I would never ask you to do anything immoral!"

"I'm glad you clarified that, Mr. Hamilton. Yes, I would be happy to show the gentleman around Washington."

"Great. I owe you one, Stephanie. Let me wrangle some tickets to a couple of shows, and of course the DHS will pick up the tab for everything."

Hennery called Tom and briefed him on the scenario, and what kind of info he wanted him to get. Hennery knew one thing; Stephanie wasn't a pro, that's for sure. A pro wouldn't have left any trace evidence whatsoever. He thought she might have done this as a favor for a friend. Maybe it's someone in law enforcement trying to be a hero. In Hennery's line of work, he met a lot of heroes, most of them were dead ones, and some he even had the pleasure doing away with himself. This hero would be no different. Hennery realized that Stephanie might have seen Tom's picture in the Dirty Dozen folder, but probably only for an instant. He was sure the hero took the file with him, so she wouldn't be caught with any evidence. She couldn't verify Tom's identity if she wanted to. It was a calculated risk worth taking.

The next day, Wednesday, January 19, was pretty ordinary. Hennery swung some tickets to a musical and a stage show at the Kennedy Center for the Performing Arts. The tickets were almost front row center; pretty good for such short notice. The performances were for Friday the twenty-first and Saturday the twenty-second respectively. He arranged for a limo, and reservations at two exclusive restaurants. He also booked a room at the Washington Hilton Hotel for Tom to make his cover look real. He told Stephanie what nights to prepare for, and what time the limo and her date would be picking her up.

Thursday, January 20, came and went. The only thing unusual was the two inches of snow that greeted commuters on their way to work. There were the usual fender benders that made tempers flare and tied up traffic. Other than that it was business as usual.

Friday, January 21, 11:00 am, Stephanie was at her desk as usual. A tall very handsome man with dark hair and a build to die for walked off the elevator and into Hamilton's office. It was all Stephanie could do to keep from staring at him like all the other women in the outer office were doing. Hamilton and the young man came out of his office and walked over to Stephanie's desk.

"Stephanie Mackenzie, this is Captain Charles Stockdale of the Royal Canadian Mounted Police."

"Charmed, I'm sure," Officer Stockdale said as he offered his hand to Stephanie.

Stephanie shook his hand and said, "Very nice to meet you."

"Stephanie, I thought it would be better if you two met before going out so you could get to know each other. Why don't you take an early lunch; extend it if you want."

"I would deem it an honor if I could take you to lunch, Ms. Mackenzie."

"Oh, call me Stephanie, Captain Stockdale."

"Only if you call me Charles."

"It's a deal. Let me freshen up in the ladies' room and I will be right with you."

Stephanie couldn't believe her luck. She was expecting some pot-bellied balding fiftyish police officer, and she got Dudley Doright, the Lone Ranger, and Zorro all rolled up in one. This was going to be one great weekend!

Monday morning, January 24, 7:00 a.m., Stephanie's alarm went off. She rolled sleepily over and turned it off. She stretched, taking in a relaxing deep breath, and then slowly let it out. Remembering the fairy tale weekend she had just experienced brought a smile to her lips.

She had enjoyed the company of Captain Stockdale very much. The restaurants and shows were fantastic. As she showered and prepared for work she went over the weekend in her head. She could have fallen for Charles, as he wanted her to call him, but she knew it was only a job, not a real romantic tryst. Actually the fact that it was nothing serious made it all the more exciting. The pressure of what to say and do to impress was nonexistent. They were just two people enjoying each other's company, and having the time of their lives on a DHS expense account. What could be better?

There were two curious things about the weekend that stuck in her mind. One, she couldn't shake the feeling that she had seen Charles somewhere before, but couldn't quite put her finger on it. Two, a strange thing happened on their second date. On their way home in the limousine they were having a glass of champagne. They decided to take a tour around Washington's landmarks because Charles was leaving for Canada on Sunday. They were parked in the limo looking at the Washington monument when inexplicably Stephanie fell asleep. She woke up ten minutes later in the same spot in the limo with Charles still sitting beside her.

She apologized to him, and he joked about it saying that he had that effect on all women.

For a fleeting moment she thought date rape, but ten minutes was hardly enough time for that. Besides, her clothes weren't even disturbed a tiny bit, and her purse was still in her lap. She had no explanation for her sudden little nap. She made a mental note that if it happened again she would have to see a doctor about it.

Monday evening, January 24, 8 p.m., Hennery drove to the office he leased for a meeting place with his Dirty Dozen operatives. He unlocked the door, turned on the lights, and went inside. He sat down behind the desk, which was the only substantial piece of furniture in the place. The only other pieces of furniture in the room were folding chairs. At about 8:15 p.m., Tom walked through the door, grabbed a folding chair, and sat down across from Hennery.

"Well, what have you got for me, Tom?"

"Everything you wanted to know, sir."

"Good, go on."

"She's had one man in her life for the past few years. He's the one that had her break into your desk. He also inquired about your schedule lately. He wanted to know what nights you worked late. He told her that soon everything wood be made public, and you would get what you deserved."

"Who is this asshole?"

"An FBI agent, Daniel Crenshaw."

"Crenshaw! I should have known!"

"You know him, sir?"

"Not personally, but I know about him. Josh Pittman told me about him, and how he doubted that terrorists were responsible for the bombings. I didn't perceive him as a serious threat; apparently I was wrong. I'll have to take some time to try and figure out what Crenshaw's plan is, and what actions you guys will have to take."

"I know I can speak for the guys when I say we're with you no matter what, sir."

"Thank you for your loyalty, Tom. So that new truth drug worked out good, huh?"

"Good? Try unbelievable, sir! All I did was put a small amount on the rim of her champagne glass, and in about eight minutes she was sound asleep and answering any question I asked. The effects lasted about ten or twelve minutes, plenty of time to get your answers. When it wore off there were no visible ill affects, and she didn't complain of any either. She didn't have a clue as to why she fell asleep, nor did she remember me asking her any questions."

"Are you sure?"

"Positive."

"OK, Tom, you can expect an extra ten grand in your pay envelope this pay day. Oh, make sure you lay low and stay away from my office. I wouldn't want Stephanie to see you, put two and two together, and tip off Crenshaw."

"Yes, sir, and thank you, sir. It's always been a pleasure working for you."

Hennery went home after the meeting he had with Tom. He had a lot of deductive reasoning to do, and his study was a good place to do it.

Hennery arrived home about 10 p.m. After exchanging pleasantries with his family, he excused himself by saying he had a lot of work to do, and retired to his study.

Hennery started thinking, *So, Crenshaw knows about the Dirty Dozen, does he? So why hasn't he done anything with the info?* Hennery thought for a while and came to a conclusion.

He's a lot smarter than I gave him credit for. He doesn't know how many people I have on my payroll, or who they are, so he can't trust just anyone. He can't go public; it's not a big enough story for the press to bother with. I'd feel in the clear if it weren't for the other things Tom had found out. Why did he want to know what days I worked late? What did he mean by everything would be made public in a little while? What would be made public? Couldn't be the Dirty Dozen, they weren't a big enough item to be news worthy. Just then, Hennery's blood ran cold, as his worst fear became reality.

Of course! The son of a bitch knows, he knows about the cable boxes! How in the hell did he find out?!

Hennery fired up his PC. Normally he wouldn't access government databases from his house, but to hell with caution now, there was too much at stake. He brought up Dan Crenshaw's service record. Served in Afghanistan Special Ops 2002 through 2004. He was stationed in Iraq 2005 through 2009.

Huh, Hennery thought, *he was in Iraq the same time I was. Wait a minute, what was that guy's name? Lorinsky's son-in-law, he was in Iraq also, I saw it when I looked up his service record.*

Hennery pulled Brad's service record out of his briefcase. *Spencer was stationed in Iraq from 2007 through 2009, the same time as Crenshaw, and look at this, even the same Ranger company. Spencer has taken up where his father-in-law left off. How they got together was anybody's guess. That didn't matter. What matters is: where are they now?*

Hennery would have to wait until morning for more info on his nemeses' whereabouts. It was too late tonight to make the required phone calls.

Tuesday morning, January 25, Hennery was at his desk bright and early researching for more info on Dan and Brad. He checked cable box recordings and found nothing. Even more proof that they knew about the cable boxes. He wondered how many people knew? He came to the conclusion that they wouldn't have told anybody for fear of a slip in front of a cable box. Probably Spencer's wife knew, and probably someone else. Hennery knew that Brad was an electronics major and army computer systems expert, but the technology behind the little black box was way over his head. He had to have had help diagnosing it. So maybe one other unknown person was involved, but that's all. That person was probably from Spencer's college. Hennery breathed a guarded sigh of relief. His guys could handle four people no matter what they had planned. Now all Hennery had to do was find them.

At 9 a.m., Hennery watched the elevator unload its passengers. When Stephanie stepped off, he watched her walk to her desk and set her purse down beside it. Then she made her way to the coffee machine and back to her desk as she always did. Little did she know what an important part she had played in Crenshaw and company's demise. Hennery made a few phone calls, and quickly found out that Crenshaw and company had taken two-week leaves of absence from their jobs. He also found out about the fourth, and quite possibly a fifth member of the group. A call to the administration offices at the college Brad was attending gave them up. It seems a Professor William Keats and his wife Keesha have taken a two-week leave of absence from their jobs. Hennery checked for recordings at the professor's home and came up with a blank.

Big surprise.

Hennery checked Keats' bio. *Graduate MIT with two doctorates: one in electronics and another in computer sciences. This guy's a fucking genius, and he'll be a dead genius if he takes part in upsetting my apple cart!*

Hennery started to think about what Crenshaw's plan would be. He figured Crenshaw as the leader because he was the only one with real field experience.

Hennery happened to glance at the clock. Oh crap, he was late for the monthly meeting with the director DHS. He would have to figure out where and what Crenshaw was up to later.

The meeting lasted until 6:15 p.m., and it was 7:00 p.m. when Hennery got into his car and headed for home. Back in his study, after supper with his family, he put on his thinking cap again. It was 9:25 p.m., and he needed a plan of action as soon as possible.

Where would they go to prepare for whatever they were planning? It would have to be somewhere remote. They couldn't risk being overheard by a cable box. Wait a minute, Lorinsky's farm! It probably has a barn, or some kind of out building where they could meet!

He checked the cable box recordings for Paul Lorinsky's house; there was nothing since the hit warning him about Paul's discovery of the black box. Even so his gut told him they were there. Hennery looked at the clock again; it said 10:35 p.m. If he called Doc and George they could be at the farm by morning. He called the two killers and told them what to do. He ordered them to observe the farm for twenty-four hours, they would observe and take no action whatsoever. They were to report back to him with what they had seen, and under no circumstances could they allow themselves to be discovered. Hennery wanted to maintain the element of surprise and secrecy until he figured out what Crenshaw and company were up to.

Thursday morning, January 27, 10 a.m., Hennery gets a call from George telling him that the suspects are getting ready to leave the farm.

"What should we do, sir?"

"I need more intel. Wait until they leave, and have a look around, but only if they're gone for good."

"Oh they're leaving for good, sir. They're taking all their gear with them."

"What have you observed so far?"

"Couldn't see much, sir, most of their activities took place in the barn, and it has no windows. They have a target range in the woods, but we couldn't get close enough to watch without running the risk of being discovered. We used a parabolic mike on the barn, and the activities sounded a lot like assault training."

"Assault training?" Hennery repeated.

"Yes, sir. Last night before they headed back to the house they discussed the mission, but not in enough detail for us to guess the target. Oh, one other thing, sir."

"Yes?"

"Crenshaw knows about Loyalty Drug 37, and he told the rest of them about it."

"Good work, guys. Now listen up. I want you to wait until they leave, then I want you to go over that place with a fine-tooth comb and find out what their objective is. I think I have a pretty good idea what it is, but I need you guys to confirm it."

"Yes, sir, will do."

Hennery leaned back in his chair; he was pretty sure of Crenshaw's target.

He's planning an assault on my offices. That's why he wanted to know what nights I work late. I wonder what he expects to accomplish? Is he going to try to coerce a confession out of me? If that's it, he's a bigger idiot than I thought. No, he may be a lot of things, but an idiot he's not. Maybe the guys at the farm will come up with something. In the meantime, I'll have to keep my eyes open at this end. I'm sure their D-day is tomorrow. They left the farm today, and I always work late on Fridays.

About 4:15 p.m. George called Hennery and confirmed his suspicions, but they couldn't figure out the details of Crenshaw's plan. Hennery called all the members of the Dirty Dozen together with a conference call. He told them to be at his office by 6:00 p.m. tomorrow, Friday, January 28, armed and ready for action.

Thursday morning, January 28, 8 a.m., Hennery was at his desk and ready to observe any early birds that came in. By 9 a.m. he hadn't noticed anything out of the ordinary. The regular nine o'clock gang started filing in. Stephanie went through her usual routine, purse beside the desk, trip to the coffee machine, coffee on the desktop, and over to his office to ask if he had anything for her to do. Then at 10:18 a.m. the elevator doors opened. A black man, dressed in light tan coveralls, carrying a black briefcase-type tool kit, walked over to the receptionist. He showed her his ID and then walked over to where the in office servers were. Hennery picked up his phone and called the receptionist.

"Who's the man in the brown coveralls?" he asked.

She said, "He was a computer tech performing a monthly diagnostic on the in-office servers."

Hennery picked up the printout of Professor Keats' bio with his picture on it.

Hennery smiled. "Well, Professor Keats, welcome to the offices of the Department of Homeland Security," Hennery said softly to himself.

Hennery watched Keats very closely from behind his desk, but not so intently as to arouse the good professor's suspicions. He mentally noted where Keats worked, and what he was doing. He stayed mainly in the server area, and used one computer near the same area. After Keats finished his work at about 11:55, he packed up his tools and headed for the elevator. Hennery let Keats leave because his appearance here meant that the assault would be tonight. He still didn't know their plan, but he was formulating an idea, and when everyone was gone after 5:00 p.m., he'd see if he was right. He didn't know just how much the conspirators knew, and who if anyone had been taken into their confidence. His plan was to take as many of them alive as he could. Then with the same truth drug he had Tom use on Stephanie, he would find out everything they knew. Then he would have them executed one by one, and their bodies disposed of in a place where they'd never be found.

Chapter Fourteen

The sign in front of the Capital City Motel flashed on and off about every three or four minutes, but the vacancy light stayed on constantly. It was Thursday, January 27, 2022, 8:25 p.m. Mary and Brad just got settled in their room when there came a knock at the door. They immediately grabbed their weapons; Brad covered the door while Mary looked out of the window to see who was there. When she saw who it was, she gave the OK sign to Brad, and he opened the door. Dan, Bill, and Keesha walked into the room.

"How do you like your room?" Dan asked.

"It's not bad, how's yours?" Brad answered.

While this small talk was going on, Bill was holding up a sign which read, "Meeting in SUV now." After a little more pointless conversation they all got into the SUV and went for a ride. Inside the SUV Bill gave everyone a startling bit of news.

"My father called me and left me a voice mail. He said a family of Islamic descent down the street from him was taken into custody in the middle of last night. No one knows where they were taken, nor heard from them since. I called my father back. He said these people weren't even practicing the Islamic faith, and they were second-generation Americans. It seems their only crime was being very vocal about the way the government is treating the people that were practicing Islam. These people told my father that they were sure the five men that confessed were coerced into confessing. When he asked how they knew they said their son who lives in Washington knew one of the guys, but that's all they were at liberty to say.

"And now it begins," Brad said gloomily.

"It would seem that our freedom of speech is slightly more than threatened at this hour," Mary observed.

"All the more reason for us to go through with our plan," Keesha added.

"Tomorrow, Bill will plant the cameras and microphones in Hamilton's office. He's the only one that's qualified to run the diagnostics on their in-office servers. How long do you think you'll be, Bill?" Dan asked.

"Shouldn't take more than two, two and a half hours tops. The cameras and mikes will not be active until you guys activate them tomorrow night. Everybody still has their pens, right?"

Dan, Brad and Mary said, "Yes."

"Any questions about the mission?" Dan asked. Everybody shook their heads no. "OK then, Brad, drive us back to the motel, and if you don't mind, I'll take the SUV and get us a little extra insurance for tomorrow night."

Dan left the four of them standing outside their motel rooms. Brad, Mary and Keesha were puzzled, but Bill seemed to know exactly what Dan was up to. Bill told the puzzled trio not to worry, it would be explained to them on the way to Hamilton's building tomorrow.

Friday, January 28, 1 p.m., Bill returned from planting the cameras and microphones in Hamilton's office. Dan met Bill outside in the motel parking lot.

"How did it go?" Dan asked.

"Smooth as silk," Bill answered.

"Great. Now take Keesha to Hamilton's building and have her drive her route at least a dozen times or more. Make sure she knows that things will look different at night. We can't afford her getting lost tonight."

"Don't worry, Keesha is a smart girl, and with the training you gave us, she'll do just fine."

"Great. Thanks for the reassurance, Bill." Both men turned and went to their perspective rooms. In a few minutes Bill and Keesha came out and left in the SUV.

Hennery Hamilton looked at the clock on his desk; it said 4:45 p.m. He called Stephanie into his office. He gave her some filing to do that would keep her past quitting time. Hennery watched each of his employees head for the elevator at 5 p.m. sharp to make the commute to their homes. At twenty minutes after five, Stephanie walked into Hennery's office and asked if there was anything else she could do? Hennery looked past Stephanie at the open elevator door, and the three men coming towards his office.

"Yes, Stephanie, I do have something else for you to do."

Hennery reached into his middle desk drawer, pulled out his forty-five automatic, and pointed it at Stephanie.

"I want you to go with these three men into the break room."

Stephanie turned to look at the three men, and immediately recognized Tom, the phony RCMP captain. She must have had a confused look on her face, because Hennery admonished her for playing amateur spy with professionals.

"Oh, don't worry, they won't hurt you, Stephanie. I need you alive and well for now." The three men took Stephanie into the break room and told her to sit and be quiet or they would gag her.

The elevator door opened again, and Zeke, one of the Dirty Dozen that built the Copley Square bomb, walked out.

"Did you bring it?" asked Hennery.

"Yep, right here."

Zeke held up an electronic instrument usually called a RF detector.

"Sweep this area here," Hennery said pointing to the areas where Bill worked.

"Nothing, the areas are clean," said Zeke.

"They can't be. Keats didn't come in here to do a diagnostic on our servers out of the kindness of his heart."

Zeke was inspecting the ventilation louvers on the doors of the server cabinets.

"You're right, he didn't do it out of the kindness of his heart; look." Zeke reached into the louver with a pair of needlenose pliers and pulled out a micro-camera and microphone.

"Good work, Zeke. Why didn't the RF detector pick them up?"

"Because they weren't active. My guess is they planned it that way, so the sniffer wouldn't pick them up. They probably planned on activating them remotely, just before they wanted them to start transmitting. They probably have a backup in case the first one failed. Yep, here's another one in the other server."

"Can you disconnect them?"

"Sure, piece of cake."

"Good, give them to me when you get them out."

"You got it."

"Oh, by the way, Keats was using this computer; check it out too."

"Right."

"Are the other guys deployed?"

"Yes, sir, they're all set to give them a fine reception."

"They do know I want them alive if possible, right?"

"Yes, sir."

The clock in the motel room said 8:30 p.m. Mary and Brad were getting their gear together. They would be lying to themselves and each other if they said they weren't nervous and scared. What sane person going into a dangerous life-threatening situation wouldn't be? Most of their gear was in a black canvas duffle bag, ready to be loaded into the SUV. They would put on their equipment after they got to their objective. Mary had to get the security guard to unlock the door, and she couldn't do that wearing a bulletproof vest. Keesha and Bill had returned about an hour ago from Keesha's orientation with the route she was supposed to drive. Just to be sure, Bill had her drive it a couple of times after darkness fell. Then they gassed up the SUV and came back to the motel. Now, they had just finished up packing and were nervously waiting for the signal to go just like Mary and Brad.

Tap, tap, pause, tap, and tap, on the door of Mary and Brad's room told them that Dan was ready for them to load into the SUV. The plan was now in motion. Even though they could still abort the mission, the thought wasn't even given serious consideration. Bill and Keesha were already in the SUV when Mary and Brad loaded their equipment in it and climbed in. The forty-five-minute drive to the target building was covered pretty much in silence. Each member of the team was going over their part of the plan in their heads, over and over again.

The SUV came to a stop in the shadow of some naked cherry trees. Dan, Bill, Mary, and Brad got out and retrieved their equipment from the back. Keesha got into the driver's seat. Bill went over to her, gave her a kiss, told her he loved her, and to be careful. She returned the sentiment, and told him to be careful too. Then she put the SUV into gear and slowly pulled away so as not to attract attention if anyone was around. The other four members of the team disappeared into the shadows.

It was 9:28 p.m. when Keesha pulled up within 150 feet of her destination. From here, she would carry her gear as close to the entrance as possible, and then con the night guard into unlocking the door for her. Just then, movement in her rearview mirror caught her attention. She looked in it and saw two dark figures slowly walking up to the SUV. They were looking around as if they were making sure she was alone. For an instant Keesha panicked, but only for an instant. Suddenly the verse from the sermon on Christmas Eve came to her, and she repeated it out loud, "Fear not, for I have redeemed thee, I have called thee by thy name, though art mine!"

Then she remembered her training. Dan had told them if you find yourselves in a defensive position try to think of a way to make it an offensive position. Always remember, the best defense is an offense. Very quickly Keesha formulated a plan. It had to be quick, because the two men were already at the SUV, one on each side.

Keesha smiled, rolled down the window and said, "I'm so glad you guys are here. I'm lost, could you tell me how to get to Thirty-ninth Street from here?"

The gang-banger looked Keesha over lustfully and said, "What the fuck do I look like to you bitch, the fucking auto club!" He opened the door of the SUV, grabbed her left arm, and started to drag her out of the vehicle.

"Get out here, bitch, we gonna party with you!"

Keesha played the helpless female to the max, begging, and putting up a token resistance. What the gang-banger didn't see was that Keesha's right hand was under a blanket on the front seat. As he pulled Keesha from the SUV, she flicked the safety off of the MP five that was in her hand, under the blanket.

The gang-banger drug Keesha clear of the SUV as his partner came around the front of the vehicle. Then Keesha made her move. She quickly brought the MP five up and pointed the barrel at the man's chest. She squeezed the trigger. The MP five burped once, and three rounds entered the man's chest, piercing his heart and exiting his back. The gang-banger was dead before his worthless carcass hit the ground. At the sight of his friend's demise, the other gang-banger was just startled enough to freeze for a few seconds. A few seconds was all Keesha needed to get to her feet. The other would-be rapist turned to run just as the MP five burped again. The running man felt three rounds pierce his back and explode out of his chest. He went down face first into a mud puddle and died.

Most women would have cried, thrown up, or just collapsed after an experience like that, but Keesha didn't have that luxury. Besides, because of her training, she wasn't an ordinary woman anymore. She dragged the bodies over to a dumpster at the side of a building, and hid them behind it. Actually Keesha was feeling pretty good right now. She had just reformed two rapists. Besides, they had their chance; all she wanted to know was how to get to Thirty-ninth Street!

Now Keesha had to get back to her part of the mission. She approached the front door of the cable office and banged on the glass doors. The guard almost fell out of the chair he was dozing in from the racket she made. He got his wits about him and came over to the doors.

Keesha put on her best sexy damsel-in-distress look, and told the guard her story through the closed doors. "My cell phone is dead! I need to call a friend! My car is out of gas! Would you puuleeease help me!"

The security guard always considered himself a knight in shining armor, so he turned off the alarm and let Keesha in. He locked the door, and turned to set the alarm when he felt an incredible electric shock and everything went black. Keesha removed the Taser electrodes from the guard's shirt, and dragged him into a side room handcuffing him to a heavy metal desk. Then she took his keys and locked the door.

Keesha went outside, brought her equipment in to the office, and carried it back to the server area. She put on the radio headset and took the front cover off of the server. She hung up the copy of the server's schematics. Bill had gone over them with her until her eyeballs ached. She did exactly what Bill had shown her to do, hooking up his equipment in precisely the right place. Now all she had to do was establish radio contact and wait for Bill's OK to proceed.

"Bill, this is Keesha, over."

Back at the target building everything had gone well so far. Mary conned the guard into letting her in, and took care of him the same way Keesha did her guard. Now all four team members were inside. Bill was setting up his laptop, TV receiver down link, and transmitter in a side room on the first floor. Dan, Mary, and Brad were putting on their equipment and checking out their weapons.

"Bill, this is Keesha, over," was heard in all their headsets.

Bill answered, "Keesha, this is Bill. Stand by to test transmission."

"OK, standing by."

Bill manipulated the keys on his laptop and asked, "Are you receiving?"

Keesha answered, "Signal verified, strong and unwavering."

"Good, stand by for clearance to transmit."

"OK, Keesha out."

"OK, it's all up to you guys now. Go get me something to transmit."

The three team members headed out the door and to the stairs. The plan was to take the stairs to the ninth floor, and then take the elevator to Hamilton's office. The reason was if Hamilton had any guards like the Dirty Dozen waiting for them; they would probably be on the ninth floor. If they took the stairs all the way to his office, they'd have twelve demented ex-CIA agents at their backs, and that wouldn't be a good thing! They would have to clear the ninth floor of any resistance before moving to the tenth floor. Actually, they weren't very concerned, because they believed Hamilton hadn't a clue they were coming.

Back downstairs, Bill was listening on his headset to the trio making their climb to the ninth floor. Suddenly his computer screen started flashing, "WARNING." Bill had placed infrared intruder alerters in the hallway outside the room he was in, and someone had tripped them! He knew that it wasn't anyone on the team because he could still hear them climbing the stairs. Bill picked up his MP five, selected full auto, and knelt down as low as he could at the door. He opened the door to just a crack, and saw two men coming out of a room down the hall with small suppressed machine guns in their hands. They were checking each room one at a time.

Bill waited until the men were in the room next door. Then he grabbed a flash-bang grenade, held down the clip, and pulled the pin. Just as they started out of the room, Bill carefully let go of the clip on the grenade so it wouldn't make any noise. He held the grenade for three seconds, then rolled it into the hall and looked away. The two men had no time to react before the grenade went off, blinding them. Bill threw open the door and opened up with the MP five. Both men were riddled with bullets before they could even raise their weapons. They dropped to the floor on their backs, never to rise again.

"Hey, team, I had two visitors. The Dirty Dozen isn't an even dozen anymore."

" Are you OK?" asked Dan.

"Yeah, I'm fine, but I think you guys might have a little more resistance waiting for you than we expected."

"Thanks for the heads up."

The team had reached the ninth-floor stairway door. Dan pushed the door open just a crack, and checked the hallway in one direction and then the other. The hall was a dead end to the right. He couldn't see anyone in either direction. Dan was the first one out of the door; he stayed low keeping his MP five up, and pointing in every direction he looked. He started moving cautiously down the hall to his left. Brad was the second one out, and followed Dan down the hall keeping the proper spacing. As previously planned, Mary would bring up the rear, and keep their backs covered.

There were five separate offices on this floor, and one single office occupying the area of five offices combined. They all had to be checked out. The first door was locked, but thanks to the guard's keys it was a snap to open. They filed into the room. It contained four desks with a computer on each desk, and filing cabinets along the walls. Slowly checking the room out they found nothing. The next four rooms proved to be the same, but the last room, the large one, proved a little different. Dan unlocked the door, and slowly opened it staying low all the way into the room. As soon as Mary got all the way into the room, she did her job and covered their backs. As she was looking at the door they had just come through; it slowly began to open.

"Behind us!" she yelled, and fired three bursts of three rounds through the door. The man trying to get in behind them fell forward through the doorway mortally wounded.

The three of them took cover behind some metal desks as a hail of bullets from five suppressed automatic weapons whistled all around them. There was a shower of glass and paper debris from computer screens and stacks of papers on the desks. Dan knew from previous experience that CIA operatives weren't trained for close-in firefights like this. That's why he concentrated the team's training on this type of fight. He signaled Mary and Brad to move up while he covered them, and then they would do the same for him. They kept up a continuous rain of fire as they advanced, keeping the five ex-CIA operatives pinned down. They worked their way to within twenty-five feet of where the five men were backed up against a wall with one door in it. Dan gave the signal for flash-bangs. He pulled the pin, let the clip fly, held the grenade for three seconds, and tossed it in the direction of their objective. Mary and Brad did the same. As soon as the grenades went off, Dan and Brad rushed the gunmen while Mary reloaded and covered their assault. Three of the five gunmen stood up and tried to fire blindly in front of them. Brad and Dan killed them before they could get off a shot.

"Weren't there five of them?" Brad asked.

Dan looked at the door to the left of where the dead trio lay; it was ajar. "They must have gotten away through there!" Dan and Brad headed for the door.

Mary was about to stand up from behind the desk she had used for cover; when suddenly she heard an unfamiliar voice say, "Freeze, assholes." Mary peeked over the top of the desk to see two men holding Dan and Brad at gunpoint. When George and Doc saw they were going to be overrun they pushed the door open and left it ajar to make it look like they had escaped through it. They hid under a table, protected their eyes from the flash-bangs, and now they had the drop on Dan and Brad.

"You guys are lucky we have orders to bring you in alive! Where's the bitch?"

Brad thinking quickly said, "She's dead, over there by the door where we came in."

"Well how do you like that, Doc? We not only knocked off the old man, but we got his daughter too."

"Yeah, go over there and make sure she's dead."

Mary had maneuvered herself unseen into a position where she could get a clean shot at the two men who had killed her father. She switched her MP five to full auto, and stood up, pulling the trigger at the same instant the barrel was pointed at the two men. She emptied a full clip into the two killers; they died standing on their feet riddled with bullet holes.

She walked over to the two dead men, kicked both of them to make sure they were dead, and said, "That's for my father."

Dan and Brad looked down at the two dead men, then looked at Mary and said, "Good job."

Then Dan said, "Now, let's go get Hamilton." Dan, Brad, and Mary got into the elevator and took it to the tenth floor. When the elevator doors opened they immediately took to the nearest cover in the room and surveyed the area. All three of them clicked the buttons on their ballpoint pen transmitters to activate the cameras that Bill had planted. The lights were on in the room, and they could see Hamilton sitting at his desk in his glass cubicle. There seemed to be no one else in the room. They stood up and carefully made their way towards Hamilton's office. When he saw them approaching, Hennery stood up, and came out of his office to greet them.

"Congratulations! I didn't think you people were that good. I guess I was wrong! You know I could find a place for you in my administration when I'm president. The pay would be more than you could imagine. How about it?"

Dan answered for all of them, "I think I can speak for all of us when I say you can take your job and shove it up your ass, Hamilton!"

"Geez, Crenshaw, I expected something more eloquent from you; your being educated and all."

"Hamilton, we know all about your bugging every private and public place in the US through the new cable boxes."

"Oh you do, do you, and what do you plan to do about it?"

"So you admit it?"

"Sure, why not? Who's listening anyway? Just you three, and who's going to believe you?"

"There's a few more than just us listening, Hamilton, and watching too, I might add."

"Oh, you mean the people listening and watching on these?"

Hennery pulled the cameras and microphones out of his pocket that he and Zeke had found earlier, and threw them on the desk that was between him and Dan.

Dan, Mary, and Brad all raised their weapons simultaneously, and pointed them at Hennery.

"Whoa there, guys! I think you better look behind you before you do anything rash."

"Mary, keep an eye on him," Dan said while he and Brad turned around to see what Hamilton was talking about. Standing just outside the break room door was Stephanie with the remainder of the Dirty Dozen. The four men had their guns trained on Stephanie.

"I know what you're thinking, but I wouldn't try it if I were you. You might get one of those guys, maybe two tops, but I guarantee you the other two will make Swiss cheese out of the lovely Miss Stephanie! Now put down your weapons and sit over there," Hamilton ordered.

Hennery pointed to three chairs set out in the middle of the floor just for them. The threesome put down their weapons and sat on the chairs provided for them. Hennery's four henchmen brought Stephanie over to them and gave her a chair also. Then all four of them were tied to the chairs.

"Now that I have you all together and comfy, let me tell you what happens next. You will be injected with a truth serum, a powerful truth serum. The lovely Miss Stephanie can attest to the effectiveness of this drug, if you have any doubts. You will tell me everything you know about anything I want to know about. Then you will all be shot in the head, and your bodies disposed of where they will never be found. I on the other hand will gain immense power from the cable box network. I'll be able to manipulate the masses, and control every man, woman, and child in the US. Hell, I can find out every dirty little secret anyone is hiding, and use it against them."

"Like you did on those guys you arrested for the latest bombings?" asked Dan.

"Yes, as a matter of fact, just like that. Hell, if I wanted to I could find out when your wife started her period," Hennery said sarcastically to Brad. "That's how personal my info can get!" Hennery paused, and looked at Dan and Brad intently. "Now I remember you two! You were in that officers club back in Baghdad in '08. You were talking about Saddam's gold cache."

"That's right, you said it didn't exist. Obviously it did, and you found it, right?" Dan asked.

"Well, since you all are going to die anyway, I might as well let you die happy. Of course I did. How do you think I financed the cable boxes?"

"Was the president or the director DHS involved?"

"Those idiots? Only in a superficial way; they had no idea where the funding came from. They think it's funds the CIA confiscated from Osama Bin Laden's bank accounts, mixed with confiscated drug money."

"Who developed that ingenious black box?" Dan asked playing on Hennery's ego.

"That was solely my idea, and Area 51 technology. The electronics designers had no idea what they were designing it for, and the manufacturers had no idea why it was on the circuit board. Perfect setup."

"Until Paul Lorinsky discovered your dirty little plan."

"Yeah, I hadn't expected someone to discover it so soon, but we took care of that pretty quickly. Now that I have the four of you, I will find out what you know, eliminate you, and I'll be home free."

"Sir. Sir?"

Tom was trying to get Hennery's attention.

"Yes, what is it?" Hennery said irritatingly. He was annoyed at his moment of triumph being interrupted.

"Sir, I just got a phone call from one of our DC operatives."

"So?" Hennery asked even more irritatingly.

"He says you should turn on the TV. That the EWS has been activated."

"What? Who in the hell did that?"

"I don't know, sir, nobody does."

Hennery went into his office and turned on the TV and the cable box. Hennery had special clearance to turn his box off, of course. When the TV and screen lit up Hennery couldn't believe his eyes.

There he was in living color and sound spilling his guts to all of Washington, and possibly the entire USA. But how! Hennery looked through the glass of his office at the cameras and microphones lying on the desk where he had thrown them.

"There must be another camera, but where?

They searched the four prisoners before they tied them up. Keats was only in the server area, and they found those cameras. Hennery's eyes scanned the office; finally his gaze came to rest on Stephanie's desk, and down to her purse.

Her Goddamn purse! She put it beside her desk every day, it was like a fixture, a part of her desk for Christ sakes. How was he supposed to notice that purse! No, he didn't make a mistake, he's not responsible, no one could have thought of that fucking purse!

Hennery went over to Stephanie's purse and looked down at it. Protruding out of the side, and aiming at where the hostages were seated was a small metallic ribbed tube. At the end of the tube was a tiny lens and microphone. The tube could be aimed by remote in almost any direction. Hennery picked up his right foot and was about to smash the camera, when he got a better idea, or so he thought.

"Give it up, Hamilton," Dan ordered. "It's over!"

"You are in no position to give me orders, asshole!"

Hennery went back to his desk and opened his middle desk drawer, took out his forty-five-caliber automatic, checked the clip, pulled the slide back, and let it go to ram a round into the chamber. Then he walked out to where the prisoners were tied to the chairs.

"Sir, what do you want us to do?" Tom asked.

Hennery looked at the four men in a daze and said, "Take off."

"Sir?"

"Take off. Get the hell out of here!"

"Yes, sir!" All four men headed for the open doors of the elevator, pushed the button for the ground floor, the doors closed, and the elevator started to descend.

Telling the four surviving members of the Dirty Dozen to leave made perfect sense to Hennery. Hennery knew he probably wouldn't survive tonight. Letting the survivors leave was one last defiant act. At least that part of his plan would live on as long as those guys were alive.

Hennery turned his attention to the four people tied up in front of him.

"You guys wanted to put me on TV and you succeeded. So I'm going to return the favor and put your execution on TV for you!"

Hennery decided to start with Mary, then Brad, then Stephanie, and last of all Dan. He wanted Dan to watch each of his team members die, so as to make him suffer the most, because after all, Dan was responsible for their deaths. He trained them and led them to there execution didn't he? Hennery raised the pistol in his hand and pointed it at Mary's forehead. Mary looked defiantly into her would-be killer's eyes. She was determined not to give Hennery the pleasure of showing any fear, or plead for her life.

Hennery was about to squeeze the trigger when an explosion blew the stairs door completely off its hinges. The SWAT team on the other side of the door had been waiting for the go signal from their commander. Their commander was watching the live feed on Bill's computer downstairs. When he saw Hennery was going to kill the hostages he gave the go signal. The door buster cannon did its work and distracted Hennery form his murderous task. The SWAT team leader told Hennery to drop his weapon and put his hands up. For one moment Hennery actually thought about complying.

Then he raised his weapon, pointed it at the SWAT team leader, and said, "Fuck you!"

The last thing Hennery heard was the bursts from the weapons of the SWAT team officers. His body shuddered from the impact of the bullets, he sunk to his knees, and fell face first onto the floor. Hennery A. Hamilton, deputy director of Homeland Security, and presidential want-to-be, was dead.

The SWAT team untied each of the hostages and verified their identity. They were taken to the elevator and down to the ground floor. Bill was waiting there with an anxious expression on his face. When Bill saw his four friends get off the elevator his look changed to a great big grin, he ran forward, and hugged each one of them.

"Is Keesha back yet?" asked Mary.

"No, not yet, but I was just in radio contact with her and she's on her way back," answered Bill.

"What about the four guys that got into the elevator?" asked Dan.

"The elevator came down, but it was empty. Believe it or not, it made no stops on the way down. They're searching the building as we speak," Bill answered.

"They needn't bother, they're long gone by now," Dan added.

"Bill!" Bill turned around and saw Keesha running up to him. She threw her arms around him and gave him a kiss.

"Are you OK?" Bill asked.

"I'm fine, but there are two gang-bangers that won't ever be the same again."

"What?"

"Don't worry, nothing happened, I'll give you the details later."

Chapter Fifteen

Saturday, January 29, 2022, 7:59 p.m., the president of the United States is sitting behind his desk in the Oval Office waiting for his cue. "Mr. President? You're on in five; four; three; two; and one."

"Good evening," the president started his speech, "by now each of you watching this broadcast over the EWS knows about the incident at the DHS office last night. The despicable acts of Deputy Director Hennery A. Hamilton of the Department of Homeland Security have been paid for by his death, and the deaths of his henchmen. This in no way excuses your president, or the directors of the major law enforcement agencies, from taking some of the responsibility for allowing this to happen. For this I am deeply sorry, and I apologize. The sanctity of the American home has been violated. As a family man myself I feel for every one of you. I know it is no consolation, but the White House was not exempt from this violation. I really do know how each of you feels. I can only say, as long as I am president, I will guarantee this horrendous situation will never rear its ugly head again.

"The director of the Department of Homeland Security has told me that an electronic bullet has been fired over the cable TV network. This bullet has permanently destroyed the black box responsible for the eavesdropping violation. Please do not destroy your cable box. The EWS works very well, and will stay in place to insure the safety of us all. You have my word that the eavesdropping ability of the box has been terminated. In order to appease those of you who may still be skeptical, there will be a short instructional video after my speech demonstrating how to remove the black box from the cable box. For those of you who are not mechanically inclined, you can call your cable provider and make an appointment to have a technician remove it for you.

"There has been some reference to a buried treasure of gold found by Deputy Director Hamilton in Iraq. I have had researchers poring over records and computer files since early this morning. So far there has been a paper trail leading to embezzlement of CIA funds by Mr. Hamilton, but no gold to be found. The development of the cable boxes themselves was paid for by confiscated illegal drug money, funds confiscated from terrorists offshore accounts, some funds from the DHS treasury, and some from the general fund. We have made those records available to the Department of Homeland Security, which is investigating the allegations. I promise that my administration will cooperate with the investigation no matter where it leads.

"It has also been brought to my attention that Mr. Hamilton's henchmen were responsible for the bombings at the Supreme Court Building, and in Copley Square in Boston. The five young men that confessed to the bombings were coerced into confessing by Mr. Hamilton using information illegally obtained by the black box. Also there seems to have been other arrests as well. I have ordered the immediate release of the five men, and anyone else illegally detained by Mr. Hamilton. I would like to convey my heartfelt apologies to those people who were illegally arrested, and to the Islamic community as a whole.

"At this time I would like to convey my gratitude to six Americans who fearlessly, without regard to their own safety, saved this nation from disaster. I am speaking of FBI Special Agent Dan Crenshaw, Brad Spencer, Mary Lorinsky Spencer, Professor William Keats, Keesha Keats and Stephanie Mackenzie. These six people, using their own resources and good old American know-how, foiled the plans of Mr. Hamilton and his henchmen. Our entire nation owes them a large debt of gratitude. I will be honoring these heroes at the White House next week with a dinner and a presentation. On that occasion, I will present each of them with the highest civilian award for outstanding achievement: the Presidential Medal of Freedom.

"In conclusion, I must convey my sincere apology again for allowing this tragedy to occur. Please believe me when I say that as long as I am president nothing like this will ever happen again. To that end, I will be meeting with James Haggerty, the director of the Department of Homeland Security, on Monday, to work out some safeguards, checks, and balances. Thank you, good night, and may God bless America!"

Monday, January 31, 2022, 8 a.m., the president of the United States is walking down the hallway to the Oval Office. His footfalls make a dull clicking sound on the highly polished floors. He says "good morning" to various members of the White House staff on the way, and in return they say, "good morning, Mr. President." He doesn't think he would ever get tired of being called "Mr. President," who would? At the doors of the Oval Office, he is greeted by two Secret Service agents with a "good morning, Mr. President." Then one of them opens the door for him. The president steps into the Oval Office and looks around. He loves the Oval Office, and especially the dark blue rug with the presidential seal in the middle. He is particularly fond of the beautiful hand-carved walnut desk, and the gold and blue draperies framing the three windows behind his desk are very appealing. He pretty much loved everything about living in the White House, and being president to the point of obsession.

The president went to his chair behind his desk and sat down. His thoughts went to poor Hennery Hamilton, a victim of his own ego. *Hennery had great aspirations; too bad he fell victim to a man with a little bit more resources and ingenuity; namely me. I find it ironic that a descendant of Alexander Hamilton would once again fall victim to a Burr. President Charles Aaron Burr to be exact! Those Hamiltons just can't seem to keep out of our gun sights; more's the pity.*

There was a nock at the door. "Yes?" President Burr asked.

One of the Secret Service agents opened the door and said, "The vice president and the director DHS to see you, sir."

"Send them in."

The vice president and the director DHS came into the Oval Office.

"Carl, James, come in, have a seat."

"Thank you, Mr. President."

"No need to stand on formality, guys. The tapes don't run until I turn them on. So how are my plans going?"

"Like clockwork, Charles. We've doubled all of Hamilton's monitors from two hundred to four hundred. We own all of them; they've all been inoculated with Loyalty Drug 37."

"Good, and the key words?"

"They've been changed, and expanded to include any criticism of your administration."

"How about the key homes I wanted monitored, like members of Congress, Supreme Court judges, the Senate, and so forth?"

"There's someone listening and watching twenty-four/seven."

"Great, you guys are great. How about the secret prisons I ordered?"

"They're being constructed as we speak, and should be in service by the end of next month," Director Haggerty answered.

"Good, we're going to need them," President Burr added. "Now, Carl, explain to me how this box works."

The vice president began with, "Charles, I hold a doctorate in electronics from MIT, and even I don't understand some of this, but I'll give it a try. This is the same cable box that Hamilton used as you already know. He had no idea that we knew of his plans from the start. As you know, we had our own technicians working on our version of the surveillance system at the same time as his technicians were working on his. The six heroes saved us the trouble of exposing Hamilton ourselves. It couldn't have worked out better if we had planned it! When we fired the bullet over the cable network we knocked out his black box and activated our system at the same time. Now, this is where it gets complicated. Let's start with the box cover.

The paint is impregnated with thousands of tiny censors forming one circuit. It goes on the principle of the shark's snout."

"Shark's snout?"

"Yes, most sharks can sense pray at great distances with censors on the surface and the inside of their snouts. What most people don't know is, the shark can also get a mental picture of their prey before they see it. Our technicians at Area 51 really outdid themselves this time. They were able to duplicate the shark's censors electronically. When mixed in paint and sprayed onto a metal surface they work together as one unit. The screws that hold the cover on connect the sensors to the circuit boards.

"Now here's were the real genius comes in. The circuit board's integrated circuits, or ICs for short, that's these little black rectangular things here, have a dual purpose. One: they process the cable information for the TV. Two: the second layer is all ours. The IC's gather our information for us, and transmit it to our monitors over the same cable as the TV. The beauty of this dual-purpose IC is that nothing looks out of the ordinary."

"You mean that there's no way the boxes' secondary purpose can be detected?" asked the president.

"Virtually impossible. With 99.9 percent predictability."

"Wow, that's impressive, and we get video too?"

"Yes, but only in the same room the box is located in."

"How about our heroes?"

"We have twenty-four/seven surveillance on them. Don't worry about them, if they so much as think suspiciously we'll pick them up and make them quietly disappear," Director Haggerty answered.

"What about the four guys that got away?" the president asked.

"The CIA has their best hit team on them; they'll be dead within a week," Jim Haggerty answered again..

"Good. Keep me updated."

There was a lull in the conversation, which was abruptly interrupted by the vice president. "Charles, I almost forgot to tell you!"

"What is it?"

"The latest polls say public opinion is holding at ninety-six percent. That heartfelt speech you made Saturday really hit home. It hit home with Congress too. For the first time since Franklin D. Roosevelt Congress is seriously thinking of suspending the two-term limit. You're on your way to a third term!"

"That was the plan wasn't it?" asked President Burr.

"Yes, sir, but the reality is a little overwhelming."

"Hey, guy, stick with me, you ain't seen nothin' yet," the president boasted. "With the info the boxes are going to provide, the sky's the limit. Just think, I'll know what congressmen and senators are going to say before they say it, and every dirty little secret they have to hide. I'll know visiting dignitaries' proposals before they ever deliver them, and personal info about each of their lives. I'll know personal information about captains of industry to use against them for donations to my campaigns. We'll nip any criticism in the bud, and we can start our persecution of that certain race of people. The possibilities are endless. With Saddam's gold and the interest it's accumulating, and that loyalty drug, we can expand our network to Canada, South America, Europe, and beyond!"

The president went to the liquor cabinet, took out three glasses, and poured three drinks of thirty-year-old scotch: all three men picked up a glass.

"Gentlemen, a toast. Today America, tomorrow the world!"

Also available from PublishAmerica

FLASHES OF SOMEONE ELSE
by C.C. Colee

Joining her friends, Maria Diaz and Rhannon Estrella, for a vacation in a quaint village in France along the Mediterranean Sea, Catherine LaRue was wondering why she agreed to the trip. The moment she arrived, she felt like a fifth wheel. While waiting in the lobby for her friends to arrive, her interest perked up as she watched a handsome man check into the same hotel. Coincidentally, the handsome man she saw that day was also a friend of Maria's who introduced himself as Cory Vann. Despite Rhannon's instant dislike to Cory, Maria continued with her silly plan of trying to play matchmaker to Catherine and Cory. It turned out to be futile as they came together without her meddling. Everything was going along just fine until one morning Catherine went off alone and took a fall. That fall would forever change her life—and that of her friends.

Paperback, 259 pages
6" x 9"
ISBN 1-4137-9166-2
Retail Price $27.95

About the authors:

Cody Lee and Chris Cole (C.C. Colee) met in the seventh grade. They have been friends for over thirty years and have always shared a love of writing. Their other works include *RB: The Widow Maker*, *RB: The Enchantress*, *RB: The Game*, *Sweet Christine* and *Casey's Soul*.

Available to all bookstores nationwide.
www.publishamerica.com